E94

THE LAST VOYAGE

This 'diary' of Captain Cook's voyage in search of the North West Passage was written as a labour of love to celebrate the bicentenary of the Great Navigator's death. For years Hammond Innes had gone out of his way on his travels to follow Cook in the remoter parts of the world. And sailing his own boats, thinking about those journals which are the impersonal records of a serving naval officer, he gradually became convinced that the only way to reveal the nature of Cook was to write the story of that last voyage as Cook might have written it had he been keeping a personal and private record of his own.

As Hammond Innes says, in presenting this book as Cook's own writing he has taken a great liberty. But he knows the sea. He knows what it is like to navigate under sail in rough weather and in fog on a rocky coast. The result is an extraordinarily gripping account of a voyage that took Cook as far north as he had been south, the first seaman to venture into the pack ice beyond the Barents Sea. And because it is a personal record, the reader is right there, standing in Cook's shoes aboard the *Resolution*.

HAMMOND INNES

The Last Voyage

Captain Cook's Lost Diary

FONTANA/COLLINS

First published in 1978 by William Collins Sons & Co Ltd
First issued in Fontana Books 1981

© Hammond Innes 1978

Made and printed in Great Britain by
William Collins Sons & Co Ltd, Glasgow

CONTENTS

INTRODUCTORY NOTE

This manuscript, which only recently came to light in the cellars of the old St James Club, is such an extraordinary document that I feel some explanation is essential. It appears to be in Cook's hand and style and covers his third voyage up to the time of his death, and to some extent it overlaps his official Journal, even to the extent of repeating passages almost verbatim. But unlike the Journal, which in the manner of those covering his earlier voyages of discovery was written more or less on a day-to-day basis, this was written spasmodically, presumably on those occasions when he had time for reflection.

As in a log, he heads each passage of writing with the day of the week and the date, and checking these against the official Journal, they coincide in the main with periods of relative inactivity. But as the voyage develops more and more of the writing seems to have been done on a Sunday, and since there is nothing in his journals to suggest that he regarded Sunday in any way as a day of rest from his main activities, I can only presume that he set this particular day aside for his private writing so that he would get into the habit of it. The necessity for this sort of discipline is evident from his official Journal, some of the passages of which are extremely lengthy, particularly those dealing with native customs and behaviour, so that he was already doing an immense amount of writing.

It has been said of Cook that, while we know every detail of his voyages, we know very little about the man himself. There are passages in this record that suggest he was in some degree conscious of this. His dislike of the two volumes Dr John Hawkesworth produced for the Admiralty from the Journal of his first voyage was such that he spent much of his time ashore after the second voyage trying to ensure that a more sensible and accurate account of his icy circumnavigation in the South Polar seas would be produced. That he should have decided to keep two journals on his third voyage – one the official record, the other a very personal account – is not, therefore, entirely surprising. He was the forerunner of all those great English writers on exploration that were to come in the next century – Livingstone, Burton, Speke, Baker, Thomson. What is surprising is the reflective quality of the writing – almost as though he had some premonition. And yet he was a man too sure of himself, and of his abilities as a navigator and a ship's captain, to contemplate death through disaster at sea.

The first page of the manuscript could be taken as an indication that the writing of it was suggested to him by Sir Joseph Banks. It appears to be a dedication of the work, but like the rough canvas cover, it has been half eaten away, probably by rodents, so that all that remains are the following almost indecipherable words –

> *This personal hist* ....
> *on board His Majes* ....
> *my third voyage* ....
>   *to J* ....
> *who made me acqu* ....
> *certain facility I did not* ....
>   *Jams* ....

In view of Cook's tendency to hark back with some nostalgia to his first voyage of discovery in the company of the young Mr Banks, and to the fact that Banks was a founder member of the St James Club, the work was most likely to have been dedicated to that 'Gentleman of Large Fortune' who was for three years – from 1768 to 1771 – his close companion on board the *Endeavour*. It was from him that Cook learned about science and the arts, and above all perhaps how to express himself. Even if it were Sandwich, First Lord of the Admiralty and his patron, who advised him to write a separate and personal record of his third voyage, it is still reasonable, and most likely, that he would have dedicated it to Banks, who was very largely responsible for his election to membership of the Royal Society Club*, an organisation for which Cook had great reverence. Certainly this would explain how the manuscript came to be in the cellars of 106 Piccadilly since Captain Gore, who brought the *Resolution* and *Discovery* home after Captain Clerke's death, noting the dedication, would have sent the bundle of papers, not to Cook's widow, but to Banks, either at the St James Club or at the Royal Society.

That it should have been left to rot in the Club's cellars may appear surprising, but it has to be remembered that at the time Banks received it he was already involved in the publication of the official account of Cook's last voyage; he certainly would not have wished the more personal journal to appear at the same time. Banks died in 1820 and under the terms of his long and complicated will he left his scientific collection and his manuscripts to his 'indefatigable and intelligent librarian', the botanist Robert Brown, for use during his lifetime, after which they were to pass to

* On the resignation of Sir John Pringle, Banks was unanimously elected President at the Anniversary Meeting of the Society on November 30, 1778, 220 Members voting.

the British Museum. When Brown finally died 38 years later the intention of the will was overlooked and much of the material never came into the hands of the Museum's trustees.

In any case, there is some mystery about the rest of Cook's manuscripts. Dr John Douglas, Canon of Windsor, who was to edit the official journal of the last voyage, was sent three parcels of writing by the Admiralty Secretary which, according to a note dated November 14, 1780, contained Cook's journal, log books and loose manuscripts. Professor Beaglehole, who spent more than thirty years of his life seeking out and examining every document relating to Cook, states quite categorically that 'all such papers have disappeared', adding, 'how and when they disappeared it is impossible to say, except that it must have been after their arrival in England.' And James King, 2nd Lieutenant of the *Resolution*, in a letter to Dr Douglas says of his search for the missing loose manuscripts, 'They are not at the Admiralty, Mrs Cook has not got them and the Clerke knows nothing about them.' He adds that Captain Gore is out of town 'but it seems unlikely that he can give any account . . .'

If these official papers could disappear under the nose as it were of ship's officers and Admiralty servants, it is not surprising that a private journal left by Cook should have gone astray. Indeed, King's Journal, covering the later part of the Voyage when he commanded the *Discovery*, has only recently come to light, having been lost among Miscellaneous Sailing Directions in the Hydrographic Department at Taunton. Nor is it surprising that, after 200 years, the condition of the manuscript is now so very bad – all the pages mildewed by damp to a greater or lesser degree, some to the extent that they are almost illegible – that without the official Journal it would have proved impossible to reconstruct. Also the manuscript itself has been worked over with many alterations and additions which have added to its illegibility. This has not made my task an easy one.

I have put it all together to the best of my ability, relying on my knowledge and fascination with the subject to fill the gaps, using for reference Cook's official Journal as edited for the Hakluyt Society by Professor Beaglehole, also the journals of those who sailed with him, Clerke, Anderson, Edgar, Samwell, and others. And in reducing and editing the volume of the writing I have followed Professor Beaglehole in omitting the profusion of capital letters which would otherwise make it difficult to read, and again for ease of reading I have split the writing up into 52 sections under my own headings; however, I have kept largely to the original spelling and punctuation so that the style of Cook's writing is preserved as far as possible.

The last twenty or so pages proved the most difficult to edit as they had clearly been written in haste and had not been worked over. This is not surprising since they cover the period when Cook had ceased work altogether on his official Journal. Professor Beaglehole writes in his Textual Introduction: 'It is impossible to believe that he committed nothing at all to paper after his entry for Sunday 17 January 1779.' This private Journal fills the gap, recording Cook's personal reactions in the last month of his life.

Finally, in my selection of what shall be included I have tried to bear in mind that this is a very personal record and the story of Cook himself rather than what he did, which has already been the subject of innumerable books.

Hammond Innes

Kersey, Suffolk.

PART ONE

A year in England

I

START OF THE VOYAGE

Monday, July 22nd, 1776

Having had a day of calm weather now after the strong gale
at South which forced me to stand to the Westward, I have
an opportunity to begin this personal history, or Diary,
of the Voyage on which we are embarked. The log book of
my last voyage closed with the words: *Having been absent
from England Three Years and Eighteen Days in which time I
lost but four men and only one of them by sickness.* In circum-
navigating the globe in those cold Southern Seas, and
thereby disproving the presence of any great continent of
land there, I thought I had been as far as a man may go.
But now that I am away in search of the North West Passage,
the which may well prove as elusive as that *Terra Incognita*
of which men like Alexander Dalrymple dreamed, I fear
I may be forced to go further than ever before. Pray God
that it will not take so many years, and that at the end of it
I may report as few men lost.

Much of my time since we sailed from Plymouth on 12th
of July has been devoted to this end, for with the Navy
committed to the disagreeable task of convoying troops to
America, the Men are not of the best and know little about
how to look after themselves. Indeed, I have only just come
from an inspection of the ship and its livestock, the which
I could not do during the gale, and having ordered the
smoking of all parts below deck and the scrubbing of tables
and other flat surfaces with vinegar and gunpowder, I took
this opportunity of demonstrating to Mr Bligh, the Master,
and some others who have not sailed with me before, my

customary routine of hygiene aboard ship and the methods I have ordinarily used to prevent disease among the men. We are altogether 113 souls on the *Resolution*, including myself and four officers, Mr Webber the painter and Omai, a native of Otaheite, also the livestock which is more numerous than on either of the two previous voyages.

During the month we were at Deptford due to delays in the fitting out and storing of the ships we had 30 desertions, all of which we have replaced. Fortunately I have with me on the two ships a dozen-and-a-half men who have sailed with me before, half-a-dozen of them on both voyages who thus have over 6 years service with me in the oceans, so that here on board the *Resolution* there has been no repetition of the difficulties experienced on the first voyage in persuading the People to a diet of portable soup, onions and fresh vegetables at regular intervals.

We were off Ushent on July 17th and 18th and are now almost across the Bay approaching Cape Finister. I intend putting into Tenerife instead of Madeira, it having been discovered that there is not a sufficiency of hay and corn on board for the animals to last us to the Cape and thinking to be better supplied at Tenerife. Thence we shall make for the Cape by way of the Cape Verde islands. I am not a little concerned about Capt Clerke, the one officer who has sailed with me on both previous voyages. He guaranteed the debts of his brother, Sir John Clerke, and on that gentleman's sailing off to the East Indies has been committed to the Kings Bench prison. If he does not get his release in time to take command of the *Discovery*, which I have left waiting for him at Plymouth having done all that is possible through my good friends, I shall not be so well served in that respect. I have every hope he may catch up with us at the Cape Verde islands or else in Table Bay where I propose to take on fresh victuals. If not, I have left orders for the *Discovery* to meet me in Queen Charlottes Sound in New Zealand which I know from past experience will provide us with all we need in preparation for our long voyage north through the Pacific.

Monday after Noon

We have on board a great deal of Instruments for Observations, more than I have had on any other voyage. As before, I am instructed to be present at the winding up of the Watch Machine, together with Mr Gore and Mr King, the first and second lieutenants, both of whom also have keys to the Box, all of us attesting the time and entering it into the Observations Book. This procedure I have just carried out, following upon the noon observation for latitude, and because all these various observations, particularly those relating to longitude, take up a great deal of my own and my officers time, I think it of some interest to list the variety of instruments delivered to the two ships.

These are:- 2 Astronomical Clocks, one with an Alarum, an Astronomical Quadrant, a Hadley's Sextant by Ramsden and another by Dolland, an Acromatic Tellescope with a treble Object Glass 46 Inches Focus, a Reflecting Tellescope, a 4 feet hand perspective with large Aperture, a Marine dipping Needle with Six Magnetic Steel Bars, 2 Small Variation Compasses, an Azimuth Compass with a spare Card, a Theodolite and Gunters Chain, a pocket Pinchbeck Watch, and Mr Bayly the Astronomer on board of the *Discovery* and I have each a small Hadleys Sextant by Ramsden as well as logarithms and a variation chart.

The Night Tellescope I shall hope to use next week if the weather serves, there being a total Eclipse of the Moon on the 30th.

It is the necessity of making continual and accurate

observations that caused me to choose in 1768 a cat-rigged collier, which was then renamed the *Endeavour*. Having been mate in these vessels and sailing out of Whitby on the Baltic coal trade before I joined the Navy as an able seaman, I understood very well their steady seakeeping qualities, they being three masted, very roomy and easy to handle. They are also shallow-draughted, enabling us to sail close inshore for the better observing of the coastline and being full-built can be readily careened, something we were very glad of after the damage we sustained when we grounded on the coral inside the Barrier Reef.

I had 2 such ships on the second Voyage, and now again I have the *Resolution* and another Whitby-built cat, the *Diligence* renamed *Discovery*. No better ships could have been devised for my purpose, except that the fitting out of the *Resolution* on this occasion has not been accomplished as well as I could have wished. The deck appears not very well caulked and after the gale on the 19th the Boatswain, who is an American named Ewin from Pennsylvania and was with me as Boatswains mate on the last Voyage, reported to Mr Bligh that there was some water in the forepart so that we had to pump. It may be that we shall discover further skimping of the work at Deptford. This poor workmanship may be due to the unreadiness of the Navy for the war against the American colonists, requiring the putting into service of additional ships and the repair of others. In the circumstances, I feel I am much to blame in that I could not look to the work myself to the extent I have done previously, the reason being that I was much engaged in the preparation of the Journal of my last Voyage for press.

There were many matters occupying my mind during the year I spent ashore between the last voyage and this. For the better understanding of the Narration I am embarked upon, I will attempt to inform the Reader of these matters later, my presence now being required on deck, and after the Cabbin will be set for dinner. Having recently butchered one of our Sheep, we shall have roast meat again today.

2

THE YEAR ASHORE

Tuesday, July 23rd

I have said I will recount what transpired ashore between my ordering the anchor let go at Spithead July 30th 1775, on completion of my second Voyage, and my finally embarking again in the *Resolution* on June 24th of this year at the Nore. If I do not do this now, and also give some account of the feeling of my Lord Sandwich and others regarding the North West Passage, it will not be possible for the Reader to understand fully the circumstances of this Voyage and my offering myself for the command of it. Also, it is certain that once we clear the Cape and head SE into higher latitudes to chart the islands the Frenchman Kerguelen visited in 1772 the weather will be of the worst and my time much taken up with the Navigation of the Ship.

At the time I completed my second Voyage I was not yet 47. I had then been 20 years in the Navy, first as an able seaman, then as Master's mate, then Master, finally as officer in command of expeditions of Discovery and Navigation. At the time of our arrival off Portsmouth I was feeling not a little anxious having returned a second time with no good report to make of that great Southern Continent of which several of my Lords of the Admiralty had entertained great hopes, believing that I would discover new and fertile lands in the Southern Ocean. Moreover, we had become separated from the second Ship under my command, the *Adventure*, off the coast of New Zealand and the last we had seen of her was at Midnight, October 30th 1773. I had heard, however, that Capt Furneaux had come safely home a year since and I now had that information confirmed and was told that the *Adventure* had arrived at Spithead on July 14th 1774.

Conscious of my duty to report to my Lords Commissioners as soon as possible, I left the *Resolution* in the charge of Lts Cooper and Clerke and hastened to London. I had much to think about on the journey, for now that I was clear of the Ship I had time to consider the reactions of the Board of Admiralty to the results of the Voyage. They would already have received copy of my Journal and the charts constructed partly from my own observations, partly from those of Mr Gilbert, my Master, also the Views, paintings and drawings by Mr Hodges and others; all these I had committed to Capt Newte of the *Ceres*, an English East India Company Ship from China which we had found anchored in Table Bay and which was bound direct for England. And by the *Dutton*, another Indiaman in whose company we had sailed to St Helena, I had sent a Packet including some of the officers journals, so that my Lords would thus be prepared for disappointment in regards to the Southern Continent.

All the information I had from Capt Furneaux since parting company with the *Adventure* was the letter he left for me at the Cape in which, apart from the loss of Ten of his best men and a boat to the natives in Queen Charlottes Sound, some of the men being eaten, he stated that he had sailed over the position of Cape Circumcision. Thus even the land Bouvet saw is proved to be no continent. And at Portsmouth I was concerned to learn that my good friend and benefactor, Lord Sandwich, was down channel sailing in a yacht accompanied by Miss Ray*, Mr Joseph Banks and others.

After being so long at sea it was not easy to adjust my mind to the hopes, aspirations and demands of those concerned with affairs of State in a Country from which I had been absent for more than Three years. There was also the matter of the book, the Admiralty requiring that the results of the voyage be presented to the Publick, but not I was determined in the loose and inaccurate manner in which the late Dr Hawkesworth had presented the first Voyage and for which his wife received the munificent sum of £6,000 after his death. I realised that I would have to look to this work myself even if there was no reward for it other than the satisfaction of the result being an accurate account and in this I would need guidance.

And there were domestic matters to occupy my mind, my poor wife not having seen me since the morning of Sunday, June 21st 1772 when I had taken leave of my Family at Mile End and gone down to Sheerness in the company of Mr Wales the Astronomer. It seemed a very long time ago, so much having happened since. And there were the two boys, James who would now be eleven and Nathanial ten. I was most anxious to see them, hoping they were in good health, remembering that three of our children had died.

On arrival in Town I went straight to Mile End, my wife overjoyed at seeing me safe at last, and everybody well and in good heart. I being a Yorkshireman and born of the land, I fear I am not of the most demonstrative, but our sense of family is very strong and it was a great homecoming;

* Martha Ray was the First Lord's mistress.

better than the last time, which was in some part over-shadowed by the death of our daughter Elizabeth only three months before, and poor little Joseph, born just after my departure dead within a month of being baptised. On this occasion there had been no such misadventures in my absence so that the reunion between Mrs Cook and myself was one of the most complete happiness and content.

That same day Mr Wales brought the Watch to London by Post-Chaise. This was the duplicate of Mr Harrisons 4th chronometer made by Mr Kendall to the order of the Board of Longitude. It had proved a most excellent timekeeper throughout the Voyage and the following day he delivered it to Mr Maskelyne, the Astronomer Royal, at Greenwich, together with his observations, which were the purpose of our taking no less than four such machines - three by Arnold, only one of which had been properly tested for a year beforehand, and one by Kendall. Testing the accuracy of all the equipment, using at times portable observatories, had taken up a deal of our time during the Voyage.

There was much to occupy me during the next few days, apart from my family, for I had to report to the various Boards, notably the Sick and Hurt Board to give an account of the crew's health and the effectiveness of such items as the inspissated Juice of wort in assisting my efforts to prevent scurvy. In this Capt Furneaux had not been so successful by failure to adhere to my practice of naval hygiene and the rigorous routine I had devised. He had been posted to the command of the frigate *Syren* and was leaving for the North American station, so I could not talk with him and had to be content with reading his journal, wishing to be assured that the massacre of his boat crew in Ship Cove had not been the result of any provocation on our part. This the journal seemed to confirm, and having in mind the warlike bearing of the natives and the trouble we had encountered on first setting foot on New Zealand in 1769, I accepted that and was relieved that he had taken no reprisals.

Lord Sandwich arrived at Admiralty House, he and Miss Ray having been so good as to leave the yacht and come to Town as soon as he knew I was returned. I spent some time with him and others, repeating to them verbally what I had already reported in my Journal despatched from the Cape regarding the Southern Continent. This I now restate for the benefit of my Readers, it being of the greatest importance that the results of so many weeks of sailing in mist and storm amongst floating ice be clearly stated and understood by the Publick:

I had now made the circuit of the Southern Ocean in a high Latitude and traversed it in such a manner as to leave not the least room for the Possibility of there being a continent, unless near the Pole and out of the reach of Navigation; by twice visiting the Pacific Tropical Sea, I had not only settled the situation of some old discoveries but made there many new ones and left, I conceive, very little more to be done even in that part. Thus I flater myself that the intention of the Voyage has in every respect been fully Answered, the Southern Hemisphere sufficiently explored and a final end put to the searching after a Southern Continent, which has at times ingrossed the attention of some of the Maritime Powers for near two Centuries past and the Geographers of all ages. That there may be a Continent or large tract of land near the Pole, I will not deny, on the contrary I am of the opinion there is, and it is probable that we have seen a part of it. The excessive cold, the many islands and vast floats of ice all tend to prove that there must be land to the South and that this Southern land must lie or extend farthest to the North opposite the Southern Atlantick and Indian Oceans, I have already assigned some reasons, to which I may add the greater degree of cold which we have found in these Seas, than in the Southern Pacific Ocean under the same parallels of Latitude. In this last Ocean the Mercury in the Thermometer seldom fell so low as the freezing point, till we were in sixty and upwards, whereas in the others it fell frequently as low in the Latitude of fifty four: this was certainly owing to there being a greater quantity of Ice and extending further to the North in these two Seas than in the other, and if Ice is first formed at or near land, of which I have no doubt, it will follow that the land also extends farther North.

To my great relief neither my Lord Sandwich, nor anybody I talked with, seemed unduly concerned that the Voyage had produced nothing in this respect to the Countrys advantage. Indeed, they had nothing but praise for the diligent manner in which I had proceeded, persevering to the limits that could be expected of both Ship and People in my attempt to discover this Land. I think it right to say that they found my detailed report more to their liking than Mr Dalrymples new book, just published, in which he had let his imagination overreach itself, still dreaming of command of an expedition and advising the setting up of a base at Cape Circumcision for the exploration of the continent attached thereto to the increase of our commerce in those parts - the very Cape the position of which Capt Furneaux had sailed over with no sight of land.

The *Resolution* was ordered up to Gallions Reach, the intention being to pay off at Deptford and lay up. On August 9th my Lord was kind enough to present me at St James's Palace where I presented His Majesty with various maps and charts. He expressed great interest in the plant specimens we had brought back, wishing that some of these should go to his gardens at Kew now in the care of Mr Banks. He also presented me with my promotion to Post-captain, I having been posted to a seventy-four, something I looked forward to with mixed feelings, never having been closer to action than when I was Master of the *Pembroke* and sounded the Narrows of the St Lawrence river opposite Quebec, so enabling general Wolfe to storm the Heights. But next day my posting was cancelled, it having been decided to lay the *Kent* up at Plymouth; as alternative I was offered the post of Fourth Captain at the Royal Hospital, Greenwich, the death of Captain Clements having created a vacancy there.

I was deeply disappointed, but on reflection my wife and I came to feel that this was for the best since it assured me of a pension of £230 per annum and free quarters with time to work on my Journal for publication. Accordingly, I wrote to Mr Stevens, the Admiralty Secretary, applying for the vacancy, but at the same time making it clear that I was ready at any time should my Country call me to more active or more essential Service, knowing myself still capable of ingaging in any duty which their Lordships might be pleased to commit to my charge. I had by then already in talk at Admiralty House had Rumour of such a duty and I had no desire to prejudice my chances of commanding another expedition, and one of such far-reaching possibilities. Mr Stevens was good enough to agree to this condition, replying that I would be employed whenever I asked to be.

So it was settled, and I had time to gather my thoughts.

Thursday, July 25th

Yesterday we had a fine gale at NNE which took us past Finister, the longitude of which Cape by the Watch and the mean of 41 lunar observations we made 9°19'12".* I do not intend to include in this Narration all our observations which are set down in the required Book, but only sufficient to remind the Reader of the purpose of the Voyage and indicate that I and my officers are constantly employed on this matter making the fullest use of the Instruments.

Capt Furneaux had brought back in the *Adventure* a native from Huahine, one of the islands which I had named the Society Isles. This had been somewhat against my wishes, knowing that this man would have to be returned there in due course. His name was Mae, but on my arrival in London I found he was known as Omai. Though far less intelligent than some that I could have delivered to London Society, he was of a most amiable disposition and had proved a great success, much as Ahutoru in Paris, whom M. Bougainville brought back. He has been presented to His Majesty, who has given him a sword and made him an allowance. He was lodged in Warwick Street, dined frequently in Society, stayed with my Lord Sandwich at Hinchinbrook Park, as well as with Mr Banks and Dr Solander, and various artists painted him, among them Mr Reynolds. They claimed he had even learned to skate. It really was most remarkable seeing him talking to the Ladies and remembering those jawbones hung up as indications of success in battle against the neighbouring islands which Mr Banks and I had seen on first going ashore from the *Endeavour* six years ago. But if any man should have been brought home by us it should surely have been Tupia without whose knowledge of those waters we should never have come safe through such a maze of islands and coral reefs.

He was in truth a strange and somewhat appealing figure,

* The actual position of Cape Finisterre is 9°18'W, so that at this stage of the voyage a considerable degree of accuracy was being obtained with the improved instruments.

being so far from his native islands and trying without any great success to behave like an English gentleman, he not having much command of the language so that I was told he addressed His Majesty as King Tosh, that being the closest Otaheitan equivalent to King George that he could manage. The truth of this I am inclined to doubt, mentioning it only to show how there were stories current about him at the time of my return, Society being not so very different from a Ship and the currency of such stories a mark of popularity.

I do not myself possess these sort of qualities of publick appeal and never have, which is something always to be regretted by those whose nature is of a serious disposition and outwardly reserved. I was never regretful of this on board my ship, for a degree of remoteness is necessary to the command of men close confined. But since I could not change my nature and habit when ashore, I had some cause for regret at that time, my introduction to Society again being not of the most successful.

I was much in demand it is true and paid the greatest attention and respect, but since it is not in my nature to be other than exact in answer to a question, I did find some time that when the Ladies enquired about even the most ordinary matters of seamanship, my explaining it to them was apparently so tedious that before I had finished they would have vanished from my side. At other times, while I was considering how I should reply to them in a manner that would be more easily understood, they would ask me about some other matter quite unconnected with the first. Something else of which I was always conscious was that, having no like background to the people I was meeting, I did not feel myself capable of engaging in general conversation and so was not at ease in their company.

I was, I must confess, more at home at the Mitre, the

tavern where the Royal Society did used to dine, and I went frequently to Jacks Coffee House and Young Slaughters to which Mr Banks had introduced me as a place frequented by artists and men of learning.

In November I was nominated for election to the Royal Society, something that was very close to my heart and a great honour. As well as Mr Banks and Dr Solander, also Mr Stevens, the Admiralty Secretary, there were no less than 22 other Members supporting me. It was March 7th of this year before I was finally admitted and in that same month my letter to the President, Sir John Pringle, on the health of seamen was reproduced in the Societys *Philosophical Transactions*. A great privilege.

Sir John Pringle, as well as being His Majestys physician, is also the authority on military hygiene and medicine. His was one house at which I greatly enjoyed dining, he being most hospitable to Mrs Cook and myself, and the discussions afterwards, and often at table, turning repeatedly to the problem of scurvy in ships at sea for long periods. We had, in fact, much to say to each other on this and similar subjects, and I greatly enjoyed these discussions, so full of facts and examples, in which I was able to explain the reasons for going ashore at each new anchorage to bring off vegetables and roots from which my crew might benefit by the improvement of their blood.

It was at one of these dinners that I met Mr Boswell, the friend of Dr Johnson, who listened most attentively to every thing I said. I met him again some two weeks later dining at the Mitre with Sir John Pringle and others of the Societys members. He seemed most anxious that I should take him on my next voyage, even though the discussion turned to cannibalism, a matter that was in everybodys mind and about which there was much curiosity after the bloody and unpleasant business at Ship Cove. Mr James Boswell was a writer with a most curious way of changing the meaning of words. At the end of the meal Sir John apologised for the poorness of it, whereupon Mr Boswell said laughingly something to the effect that he had had an excellent dinner because he had had a good cook, and he pointed at me, meaning I suppose that he had enjoyed our conversation. Everybody laughed heartily at this and we went on to Browns for coffee and then to the Royal Society.

Four days later he called upon me at Mile End, Mrs Cook giving us tea in the garden, and we talked for some time. Later he presented me with a signed copy of his book *Account of Corsica* in which he had written: *Presented to Captain Cooke by the Author, as a small memorial of his admiration of that Gentleman's most renowned merit as a Navigator, of his esteem of the Captain's good sense and worth, and of the grateful sense which he shall ever entertain of the civil and communicative manner which the Captain was pleased to treat him.* I read the book immediately for what I could learn from it as to the best way to present travel to the Publick, it then being April and myself deeply engrossed in my own work, which I found no easy matter, the manuscript already so full of alterations and additions that it was difficult to read.

Wednesday, July 31st

We have been on deck the greater part of the night observing the Eclipse of the Moon through the Night Tellescope. By this means, and the use of the Ephemeris tables, our longitude was 15°35′30″, whereas by the Watch it was 15°26′45″. Clouds hid the Moon the greatest part of the time, particularly during the beginning and end of total darkness, so that our observations were not of the best. Tomorrow we shall anchor in Tenerife if the wind holds and there being much to do there, including the procuring of water as well as hay and corn and other articles we are in want of, also a description of the place to enter in my official Journal, I must now take this opportunity of giving some account of the work that occupied so much of my time ashore before the start of this Voyage.

Dr Hawkesworth, having died of a slow fever three years ago, I was spared the possibility of the preparation of my Journal being offered to him. In his account of the first Voyage, which I read at the Cape outward bound on my second Voyage, I found he had quite disregarded all my amendments and requests. He knew little of seamanship or navigation, had no knowledge or interest of the world I had explored, yet wrote as though he was the very person in command. A strange mannerism which I found most mortifying. And he adopted this mode of writing, not for my own Journal alone, but also for those of the other commanders* which were the subject of the first of his three volumes. He spoke thus with several voices, but it was all the same, his endeavour to entertain and thereby attract the attention and support of the Publick involving flights of fancy so that both I and the officers were for ever saying things we would never have said and in a manner foreign to us.

I was determined that this time the work should not get out of my hands. But I am not myself a writer, though I know very well what I wish to say and can set it down after a fashion. Three years in the Great Cabbin of the *Endeavour* in the close company of such learned gentlemen as Mr Banks and Dr Solander had much improved my ability to express myself. Whether my Lords, conscious of my lack of suitable education, had in fact proposed that Mr Forster should have charge of the work I do not know, but certainly that would appear to be his impression. Indeed, he went so far as to

* The first volume of Hawkesworth's *Voyages* comprised three earlier voyages, those of Byron, Wallis and Carteret.

declare that he had made it a condition of his sailing with me on the second Voyage that he should write the history of it, receiving all the profits from the work in addition to a pension and the £4,000 voted by Parliament for the support of a man of learning on the expedition.

John Reinhold Forster had been recommended for the position by the Hon. Daines Barrington* after Mr Banks, Dr Solander and Dr Lind had all withdrawn from the expedition, the first in some dudgeon because he could not have the command of it. Many times during the voyage I had recalled with some nostalgia the pleasure I had had of the company of Mr Banks and Dr Solander in the *Endeavour*, and to have them replaced by this tedious, talkative, self-opinionated man so full of his own importance was hard to bear. And then, when we returned, to be faced with his arrogant demand that he, not I, should be in charge of the preparation of what was my own work. However, my Lord Sandwich conceived a neat solution to the problem. He requested Mr Forster to submit as an example of his work an account of our sojourn in Dusky Bay, that grim, forbidding inlet in the SW of the Southern island of New Zealand. He was given that section of my Journal to combine with his own recollections, and though it is generally supposed he got his son George Forster to do the writing, the specimen he finally produced proved less than satisfactory and was rejected.

This was in October of last year and I fear it was a terrible blow to his Vanity, for he at once indicated to Lord Sandwich that he could not be held responsible for the inaccuracies and vulgarities of expression he had found in my Journal. Lord Sandwich wrote immediately in my defence and afterwards there was some talk of a joint work, myself dealing with the navigation and Forster with the botanical material. But having lived with the man for so long I knew

* A member of the Board of Admiralty.

he would hang himself with the rope he had been given, and so from that moment I proceeded to work on the book in the certain knowledge that I should be sole author of it.

And so it turned out. But I was not so sure of my ability in this respect as to think it could be carried through without guidance. I discussed this with Lord Sandwich and he, having agreed, at once asked the Revd John Douglas Canon of Windsor to be my tutor. It is one thing to write day-to-day reports for their Lordships, quite another to prepare those same reports for press, even though they have been written in the form of a Journal. I have no proper command of grammar, spelling or punctuation, and for the Publick the work needs to be divided up into chapters, the longer sections into paragraphs, sentences shortened, and some rearrangement made in certain passages to give the Reader a sense of order. In part I was able to do this myself, but it would not have been so well done without the guidance of Dr Douglas, who was most helpful and painstaking, ensuring that any mention of the Amours of the People shall be unexceptional to the nicest of my Readers. And though His Majesty knew he was helping me, I do not think anyone except my friend Dr Shepherd was privy to the arrangement, Lord Sandwich making it very clear that it was best kept private. I think he was afraid Mr Forster would hear of it, he with his son George having been with me as naturalists and presuming he would have the writing of it. By then I fear my Lord Sandwich had had more than enough of that gentleman. Indeed, he once asked me how I had suffered him for three long years, but I said I had other matters to occupy my mind and scarcely noticed his presence after the first few days. The fact is that close contact with others and shipboard routine forces a man to keep a tight hold on himself. Forster was not a tenth as tiresome on the *Resolution* as he was ashore, perhaps because, like all of us, he had a settled position whilst he was on the Ship and work to occupy his mind.

That every man on board has activities to occupy himself even on long voyages seems to be something difficult of comprehension to those I talked with who have not been to sea. My attempts to answer them appearing tedious, I found they understood more readily when I indicated the crafts and trades represented on board. For example, on this voyage our total complement at present on board the *Resolution* is 114, which must appear a great number considering the size of the Ship and its ease of handling, but is not so great when it is understood how much of stores and gear must be seen to.

For the sailing of the ship, apart from myself and the 3 officers, Lts Gore, King and Williamson, there is the Master, Mr Bligh, 3 Masters mates and 50 able seamen. Of these last, 2 do duty as gunroom servants, 2 more are in the carpenters crew, one acts as cooks mate and Benjamin Lyon I can call upon when there is anything wrong with the Instruments, he being a trained Watchmaker. Also we have 7 midshipmen, and of course Mr Anderson and 2 surgeons mates. The Supernumaries on this voyage number only two, Mr Webber and Omai.

For other duties we have 5 Quartermasters, a Boatswain and 3 mates, the Gunner with 2 mates, a Sailmaker and 1 mate, a Carpenter and 3 mates, a Cooper and Ships Corporal, and the Armourer and his mate. Besides which there is my Clerk, Alexander Dewar, and my servant, William Collett, who is also the Master at Arms. These are the men who look to the well-being of the Ship. For guard duties and for the maintenance of good order, and also for a disciplined show of our strength whenever it may be necessary among native peoples, we have a Sergeant, 2 Corporals and 16 privates of the Marines under the command of Lt Phillips.

All these men, together with our great quantity of stores, and also our livestock, would seem to make for some congestion on board. But they all have their place and duties, and with the seamen split into watches, so that there is never a time except in port when all are below, most do normally have more than the Navys allowance of fourteen inches space for each mans hammock. And the situation will be much improved when we are in warmer seas and many can find a place on deck to sleep without too great a disturbance. We had more on board last voyage and no complaints about conditions below, except the usual of wet quarters upon occasion.

3

A NEAR DISASTER

Monday, August 5th

We were in Tenerife some three days, anchored on the SE side of the Road of St Cruz. Being half a mile from the shore there was much work for the boats crews. I bought live bullocks, other cattle and poultry, also pumpkins, onions and potatoes which are the best keeping I ever had, but could wish for the Wine being near as good as that of Madeira, which it is not, though less than half the price at £12 a pipe. Of particular interest to me was the presence in the Road of the French frigate *Boussole* Capt Bourdat* command-

---

* His correct name was Jean-Charles Borda. He was well known as an experimental physicist and mathematician, also as an inventor of mathematical instruments.

ing, one of that Country's best navigators. In conjunction with a Spanish gentleman, Mr Varila, they made observations from a tent on the pierhead, comparing the Watches they had on board every day at Noon with the Clock on shore by signals.

Capt Bourdat was good enough to communicate these signals to us so that we could compare our Watch. The result was the same longitude within a few seconds, confirming that our Watch had not materially altered its rate of going. This is something that affords me considerable satisfaction for where we are bound on this voyage we shall have much need of an accurate timekeeper and no means of checking it. I have detailed all this more fully in my official Journal, being told by Dr Douglas that I should not in this more personal record involve my readers too much in the observations, they not being greatly interested in such information. This is something I find hard to understand, my whole life being so much taken up with astronomical observations and the mathematics of precise navigation for the purpose of determining my position accurately at all times and so drawing my charts correctly. Sufficient to say here that Capt Bourdat is charged with determining the exact position of the Peak of Tenerife.

I could have wished we had more of each others language, but not withstanding this difficulty I did enquire of him the latitude and longitude of the island his compatriot Capt Kerguelen had sighted in the S. Pacific and he did give it to me. It was not the big island, but a smaller island he had named Rendezvous. Its latitude by seven observations was 48°26'S and the longitude by the same number of observations of the distance of Sun and Moon was 64°57'E of Paris. By this means I shall be able to close the island even in Fog so long as I can obtain the observations required to establish my own position.

We weighed anchor yesterday, our course after clearing Tenerife SSW and helped on our way by a fine gale at NNE.

Sunday, August 11th

It is now 22 minutes after midnight and I have been on deck for the past 3 hours, the situation being for a short time most hazardous, and my own fault for believing we were well to the E of the Cape Verde islands with open water ahead of us. While I was here in the Cabbin writing my Journal, which I had been since shortly after sunset, I was conscious latterly of an increasing sense of unease. This is something that I have learned never to disregard for it has many times saved us from danger, though not on the occasion of our grounding on the Barrier Reef when I had no such feeling but was fast asleep.

I had left the navigation to Mr Bligh*, who at 21 may be regarded as very youthful to be Master, but he has proved a most excellent navigator and seaman, as indeed he was recommended to me. This unease that I have sometimes felt is a most strange thing, very common among masters and captains who have spent long periods at sea in the same ship. It is as though Captain and Ship were one and the Ship a sensient being aware of danger and capable of communicating the awareness to the one person who can order action to avert it. The interest of writing caused me to ignore the message I sensed in the movement of the Ship and the sound of its timbers, so that I had almost left it too late, wishing to complete the official Journal to this date and continue my explanation of how it transpired that I was able

* William Bligh, notorious for his command of the *Bounty*, a brilliant seaman and navigator whose appointment as Master at such a young age and after only 6 years in the Navy is surprising and remarkable.

to prepare my Journal for press and the guidance I had from Dr Douglas.

After the lamplight in the cabbin it was a little while before I had accustomed my eyes to the darkness on finally going on Deck. We were continuing on our course of SSW and I was peering to starboard, when suddenly land was sighted over the bow and I made out the unmistakeable shape of Bona Vista island. I had not forgotten the SW-going current to be expected in the neighbourhood of the Cape Verde islands; indeed, I had warned Mr Bligh before going below, but either our position by the Watch at the noon observation was at fault or the set of the current was a good deal stronger than I had believed possible.

It is likely that both affected the present position of the ship, for on hauling to the Eastward, which was the best we could do to get out of the danger, it became clear that we could barely make enough speed through the water to counteract the current setting us down on to the island, and we had a very unhappy three hours of it, the island getting nearer all the time. Even when we appeared to be clear of it, this proved not to be the case for I saw my surgeon, Mr Anderson, standing at the starboard rail staring intently and when I joined him I also made out a loom of white extending beyond the last headland, which was the break of waves on a reef lying to the SE of the island.*

Our situation for a few Minutes was very alarming so much so that I did not dare sound the bottom for fear that the rocks would be as close under the keel as the coral had been on Endeavour Reef and that the leadsman crying the depth should cause so new and inexperienced a crew to lose their nerve. For those few Minutes I held my breath, as I imagine did the other officers, the white of breaking waves

* This reef, called Domingos dos Sentos or Ninho do Guincho, extends some 2¼ miles south east of Bona Vista.

so close in the darkness and audible over the sounds of the ship driving through the water. Once we were clear, I noted that Mr Bligh was shouting his orders very loud, which though natural was regrettable, all of us feeling that same sense of relief, but not expressing it.

Now that I am back in the Cabbin again and the ship on its proper course of SSW I must give some thought to the Cause whereby the ship was put in a position of such hazard. I have not spoken with any of the officers on the matter, wishing them to regard it as of less importance than I know it to be. No doubt I have become so accustomed to this run down the Atlantic that I take our safe arrival at the Cape for granted. But to run so close to the Cape Verdes, presuming upon the accuracy of my position, and thereby placing ourselves at the mercy of the current, is something outside of my normal practice.

Is it that I have become too accustomed to relying on my officers and particularly the Master, being so well served on my last Voyage? Or have I become less careful? If it is myself that is to blame in that I have become over-confident as the result of having been in so many dangerous seas and brought my ship through safely, then that is a serious matter that can be attributed to nothing less than some fatigue of the mind. So often I have seen bodily tiredness lead to a lack of mental alertness. I do not feel tired, though the last year has been a very full one and not at all easy. I recall that my Lord Sandwich and others of the Admiralty were most considerate in not proposing me for this command, but waited upon my offering myself, whereupon they accepted, seemingly with great relief.

I was certainly a tired man when we emerged from the Southern Seas more than two years ago now. We were altogether sixty six days south of Latitude 60°, reaching as far south as 71°10′ on 30th January 1774, and during all that time I had very little sleep being constantly on deck. But I had fully recovered by the time we had completed the long voyage home from New Zealand. Indeed, it seems that I was looking a deal better than when I had left three years before, Dr Solander saying so in a letter to Mr Banks who passed on to me the good doctors estimate of my state of health, seeming much pleased that I was so full of vigor. But since then I have had much to do.

Apart from the preparation of my Journal, and all the difficulties with Mr Forster who was cutting his own throat and blaming everyone else, there was from as early as mid-December of last year the business of searching for a ship to accompany the *Resolution* on the Voyage, their Lordships having entrusted me with the finding of it. And about that time my wife discovered herself to be with child again. My dear Elizabeth is such a very comfortable, easy, companionable person, so efficient a housekeeper and so uncomplaining, that at no time did she give me any cause for alarm. But the fact is that this little boy, who was born only a few months since in May and baptised Hugh, though the fifth of my children, is the first at whose entry into the world I have been present. And knowing by then that I was shortly to leave on a further voyage I think we both had cause for feeling closer than ever to each other.

This is not a matter that should in any way have exhausted me, but it added to my responsibilities at a time when I was deeply committed to other activities, not least to my election to the Society and my writing of the paper on Hygiene at sea. And there was that dinner my Lord Sandwich gave when I said I would command the expedition with all the resulting letters and organisation, as well as the tiresome business of sitting for my portrait by the painter Mr Dance, which was kindly commissioned by Mr Joseph Banks, in admiration of me, he said.

All together there was so much to do, so many demands on my time and energy, that I may well be more tired than I feel myself to be. And then to find the ship ill fitted out and leaking, Clerke in prison and the *Discovery* left to follow after us. I must now watch myself, keep a hold on my temper and curb that irritableness which Mrs Cook has so often remarked upon. But at least I am not of a melancholy disposition though sometimes accused of it, those who do not like me mistaking silence and an inclination to careful thought for that condition of mind.

PART TWO

Down the Atlantic again

4
RUSSIAN MAPS

Friday, August 30th, 1776

Now at last we have picked up the Trade Wind, the interval since I previously wrote being full of disappointment and frustration. At day break following our being set so close upon that reef I hauled to the Westward to pass between Bona Vista and the isle of May intending to close the island of St Iago, I having told Capt Clerke he could meet up with me there at Port Praya. In this way we had sight of the rocks we had so nearly gone down upon and during that day and the next we made every attempt by sounding to determine the rate of the current, which we found to set SWbyW something more than half a mile an hour. We were off Port Praya at 9 o'clock in the morning of Tuesday 16th, there being 2 Dutch Indiamen anchored there, also a brig, but no sign of the *Discovery*, and having expended but little water we stood on to the southward.

We now lost the NE trade and there followed more than two weeks in which the condition of the ship rendered living on her very unpleasant, the wind being from SW blowing some times fresh and in squals, the weather generally dark and gloomy with frequent rains. These rains enabled us to fill those water casks that were empty, but that was all the good we got of them, the ship proving extremely leaky in all her upper works, the hot dry weather we had recently experienced having caused the bad caulking of the deck to open up, even the sides of the ship, so wide that the water came in as it fell. Not a man had a dry bed and the officers in the gunroom driven out of their cabbins.

It is on this passage that I find it particularly necessary to be on my guard against disease by obliging the people to dry their cloathes and take every opportunity to air the ship with fires and smoke, which is never to their liking. I am glad to say that as a result of this, and despite the leaking of the ship, I have fewer men sick than on either of my former Voyages. And we had fresh fish, Omai proving very apt to the sport, catching twice as many of the small dolphin* that were about the ship than anyone else he using a rod with a white fly.

Unfortunately, there was little we could do about the sails, they being very wet with the water getting in to the sail rooms and some quite ruined. Having experienced this problem on my previous Voyage I had made representation to the yard officers at Deptford, who undertook to rectify the matter, but it would appear that either my representations were ignored or the work skimped. We shall I have no doubt a great deal of trouble with the Canvas and the sailmakers much unnecessary work in the future. And now that we have the SE trade and conditions more settled the caulkers are set to work caulking the decks and the inside Weather works of the Ship.

Having done all that is possible for both Men and Ship, I shall now have some time to write about the purpose of the Voyage and what I did while I was ashore to prepare myself for it. This being quite different to my official Journal I shall keep under Lock and Key, for I have no intention that the men shall learn about my innermost thoughts, and the knowledge that our ultimate destination is into the ice of the North Polar regions would be the surest way to induce desertion once we are in those friendly and hospitable

* This is almost certainly the true dolphin, which is a fish found in warm waters, not the relative of the whale which we generally call dolphin.

islands of the Pacific. Ignorance of my intentions is I am convinced the best safeguard against the need to exercise the full penalties of Naval Discipline, something I am always willing to do for the good of the Ship and her People, but which I know from my own experience in the lower decks is in some degree to fail in the proper leading of the men under my command.

But I must leave this for the moment, it being close on Noon and my presence on deck being required for the Azimuth . . .

Saturday, August 31st

It is six months since I wrote that letter in the Admiralty office formally offering myself for command of the expedition, the which I had already and perhaps rashly done at my Lord Sandwich's dinner table. Between that date and the start of the Voyage among other matters that occupied me was the necessity of learning everything possible about the seas to which I have committed myself, my officers and my men, and to gather together such maps as exist, which is very few. This, as has been evident in the recent rains, proved greatly to the disadvantage of the Ship, for together with the preparation of my Journal, it left me little time for looking to the fitting out, victualling and all the other matters to which I have usually given close attention.

But first I must explain why I offered myself for the Voyage, or perhaps it would be more honest to say that I must now endeavour to explain it to myself, for now that I contemplate setting it down I find myself in some difficulty since I am not sure what it was that induced me to leap to my feet at the dinner table, fired by the nature of the arguments, hopes and speculations, to announce to the others, they being my Lord Sandwich, Sir Hugh Palliser, the

Comptroller of the Navy Board, and Mr Stevens, the Secretary, that I would take command if that was their wish.

Undoubtedly it was to some extent due to the feeling that prevailed on this matter of the North West Passage at the time of my return to England last August, particularly among the Members of the Board of Admiralty, the Government and the Royal Society. Since the arrival of the *Ceres* from the Cape with my Journal all had known that there was no Southern Continent offering the prospect of increased trade. This hope being finally dispelled, and the Prime Minister, Lord North, himself ignoring Mr Dalrymples request to be sent out at his own expense to colonise the Isle of Georgia* discovered by the *Leon* in 1756 and which I had described in such terms that made the prospect of colonisation unthinkable, all eyes were now turned once again to the North Polar regions and the question of the Passage through between the Atlantic and Pacific oceans. Such a passage for ships trading to China, the Indies, and all the islands of the Pacific I had claimed for the Crown would be of great advantage to the commerce of our Country.

Belief in the existence of this Passage was of long standing. They tell me it is referred to in a posthumous Hakluyt which claims that a Greek pilot, Juan de Fuca, was sent in search of the Passage which was then called the Straight of Anian. North of Lat.47° on the west coast of America he entered an inlet and after sailing for 20 days came out into the Atlantic and then sailed back again through this same passage. According to the Notes I have made, this was in 1592 and was the origin of this belief, which was held so firmly that in 1670 the search for it was written into the Charter for the setting up of the Hudsons Bay Company.

* The name Cook gave to South Georgia.

Saturday evening

The men who have searched for this Passage are very numerous. They include Frobisher, Davis, Hudson, Baffin. But except for Sir Francis Drake and some others, including the Spaniards sailing north from the Pacific ports of their American colonies, they have all approached it from the Atlantic. And the Hudsons Bay Company has only recently, and that under the strongest compulsion, undertaken exploration with this in view, and then all of them by land, except Govnr James Knight who took 2 ships up the west side of Hudson's Bay but found no tide to sweep him through to the Pacific. Though he lost his life in the attempt I do not think he was very serious in his endeavours being more interested in gold.

I did myself make representations to the Company, both personally and through my friends, but like the East India Company and other big City of London adventurers they proved most secretive, only pointing out that their Govnr after Knight, Henry Kelsey, got further than any man before him across the North American continent, but that there is no great hope of a sea route, the land being very bleak in its northern parts and Ice most months of the year. Kelsey wrote a Journal, the which an Irish gentleman Mr Dobbs has in his possession, this being the origin I am told of his extreme interest in the Passage.

It was Mr Dobbs who persuaded the Admiralty to obtain Royal consent for a naval expedition. This was in 1741, he having written a memorial on an easy sea route to China ten years before. Capt Middleton, late of the Hudsons Bay Company, was employed in this venture, but found the current from E and no way to the Westward from Hudsons Bay. And then in 1745 Parliament enacted a reward of £20,000 for the discovery of the Passage and some London merchants tried but failed. Finally one of the Companys servants, Samuel Hearne, put an end to hopes of a passage from that direction by journeying overland from Fort Churchill at the bottom of Hudsons Bay to the North Polar Sea without crossing any river or salt sea passage.

As with that great Southern Continent, *Terra Incognita*, de Fucas passage through the North American continent would appear another dream of those geographers and map-makers who let hopes rather than observations direct their pen. Nonetheless, Mr Daines Barrington, who is a member of the Council of the Royal Society and a friend of my Lord Sandwich, believes in it absolutely, so much so that in December of last year he persuaded Parliament to extend the Act offering £20,000 to him who first discovered the Passage and he also persuaded them to include a reward of £5,000 for all the People of the first ship to sail within 1° of the North Pole, being I fear one of those who believe that there is not any ice in the North Polar sea.

This matter of reward was the subject of some conversation between Mrs Cook and myself, since were I to discover the Passage it would be to the considerable advantage of all our household. I was never at any time offered any personal inducement, but in conversation with my Lord Sandwich and others before I even offered myself for the service, it was understood that whoever was successful would not be lacking advancement and afterward it was repeated. By which I understood there would be promotion from my present rank of Post-Captain and Sir John Pringle also hinting to me that there would be proper recognition of the achievement, I took him to mean that my service would merit some honour, the which I understood an honour bestowed by His Majesty.

Now that I am at sea, so far on my voyage that tomorrow

we shall cross the Equator, I find I view this matter somewhat differently, being conscious of the Difficulties and Hazards that lie ahead. But at home in Mile End discussing it with my dear Elizabeth the prospect of position and the monies to uphold it quite dazzled us both. She, however, thought nothing of it so much as the danger to which I might be exposed and I do not recall that she expressed anything more than satisfaction that my Voyages be afforded proper recognition.

Thus I can say that it was not she who persuaded me to offer myself for the command of the Voyage. Nor I truly believe am I ambitious of such recognition or particularly desirous of the rewards. It was the challenge and the distress I felt ashore that my capability in Navigation was not being used for the service of my Country at a time when we were at war. It was not a sudden decision, though it may well have appeared so to Lord Sandwich and the other two gentlemen being entertained by him that day, but was come to gradually so that my leaping to my feet and declaring I would go if they so wished was well considered beforehand if abrupt in the stating of it.

Sometimes when I am alone in my cabbin I think about this and wonder if I was right. And since I never did such a thing before, accepting all my instructions as part of the service for which I had volunteered those years ago, I fear it is a mark of age. This Voyage will see me past 50 and approaching that I am aware that my mind is become more reflective, to which I attribute my committing my thoughts to paper in this way, something I would never have done when I was younger.

Now I must turn the Readers attention to the Russians, who for more than a century past have interested themselves in the northernmost part of the Pacific. The first voyage of discovery they undertook proved that Asia and America were not joined in the upper part, but the mapmakers taking no note of this the Czar ordered a ship out of the Kamtschatka river commanded by Behring who was a Danish captain in their service. He reached latitude 67°18'N and having no sight of the North American land presumed he was in a strait separating the two continents. This strait is shown in a map contained in a new book published 2 years since, also the many islands some of which Lt Sindo reported on his voyage some years ago.

This book, called *An Account of the New Northern Archipelago, Lately Discovered by the Russians in the Seas of Kamtschatka and Anadir*, was brought to the attention of the Royal Society by the Secretary, Dr Maty, and an English translation having been made, I have it with me on board together with the map. It is the most recent and accurate I can get, including the observations of Behring and Tschirikow sailing from Petropaulowska in 2 ships. I also have on board the older book *Voyages from Asia to America* which includes a map showing Behrings first voyage, also that of Gvodzev, and was translated to English in 1761. Among the other maps I have are 2 French and John Greens of 1753.

But the map I must rely upon, in so far as I dare, is the new one, which the Society referred to me as the Stählin map because it was first printed by Jacob von Stählen of the German Academy of Sciences. It is much to be preferred to the Müller of 1758, being more recent and showing the NW coast of N. America much broken with islands, the largest of which are called Alashka and Unalashka, and there is also a line of smaller islands named Aleutskia.

5

CROSSING THE LINE

Wednesday, September 4th

We crossed the Equator last Sunday and those who regarded themselves as veterans of the Equatorial Line, having for the most part crossed but twice on the outward and homeward passage, did see to the Ducking of all those who had never crossed it. I know Capt Clerke will have none of it if he is on board the *Discovery*, issuing Grog by way of compensation, and my surgeon, Mr Anderson, has expressed a strong view of this in my hearing, supported by Mr Bligh to my great surprise. But it is the custom and to my thinking customs are important, giving some opportunity for merriment among the men. That there is some danger in it I do not accept, believing there to be as much hazard to the Ship and her company in the issuing of spirits, there being at the time a gale from SEbyS.

I well remember Mr Banks being greatly shocked at the state of our crew during Christmas Day 1768 when we were running down towards Cape Horn, he noting that by night fall all the crew were 'abominable' drunk and declaring his thanks to God for a moderate breeze since if it were otherwise he did not know 'what would have become of us, there being scarce a man sober enough to work the ship.' He did of course not fully understand how very easy these vessels are to work and that the officers could readily have handled her if the need arose.

I believe altogether upwards of 40 men were Ducked. All I wish to say on this matter is that men who have to live for months, indeed several years, close confined within the

53

wooden sides of their ship are subject to as much despair, disaffection and enmity as any like number of prisoners, so that unless they are afforded excuse and opportunity for the release of their spirits they will make trouble. And this being something I do my best at all times to avoid, I consider it no advantage at all to save some from discomfort at the hands of others when all expect of the crossing of the Equatorial Line a day of frolicking. It is a break in the shipboard routine, they behaving like children let from school and the officers like tutors keeping as much apart from the activities as is conducive to the safety of Men and Ship.

During the last week or more we have had the pleasant distraction of watching the flying fish so common to this area and when we can catch them they are very good eating. We have also had a great number of porpoises around the ship which pleases everyone, also bonitos, puffins and boobies, and the men have had some sport catching sharks. Two days ago, and again this evening there has been a great display of luminosity in the water, the phosphorous clinging to the sides of the ship and to anything, even a line, that is wet. This is the same we saw in the *Endeavour* when there was great discussion as to the cause of it. But here again Mr Anderson, who is much interested in Natural History and has made a study of it, could find no small sea creature in the water that was lifted on board to explain it.

6

SECRET INSTRUCTIONS

I believe this to be the most convenient place in the Narration to direct the Reader's attention to the Secret Instructions, which were delivered to me in a sealed package on board the *Resolution* at Plymouth by Butler, the Admiralty Messenger, on July 6th, four days before we sailed. Without sight of these the direction I am taking to achieve the primary object of the Voyage would not be clear. A copy of these Secret Instructions was also delivered to the *Discovery* with a note to Capt Clerke that he was not to open them unless he failed to meet up with me at any of the ports at which I had left orders for him to meet me.

*Copy of Secret Instructions made by me
off the Coast of Brazil
Wednesday, September 4th*

By the Commissioners for executing the Office of Lord High Admiral of Great Britain & Ireland &ca

*Secret Instructions for Capt James Cook
Commander of His Majesty's Sloop the Resolution*

Whereas the Earl of Sandwich has signified to us His Majesty's Pleasure that an attempt should be made to find out a Northern passage by Sea from the Pacific to the Atlantic Ocean; And whereas we have in pursuance thereof caused His Majesty's Sloops Resolution & Discovery to be fitted in all respects proper to proceed upon a Voyage for the purpose abovementioned, and, from the experience we have had of your abilities & good conduct in your late Voyages, have thought fit to intrust you with the conduct of the present intended Voyage, and with that view appointed you to command the first mentioned Sloop, and directed Capt Clerke, who commands the other, to follow your Orders for his further proceedings; You are hereby required and directed to proceed with the said two Sloops directly to the Cape of Good Hope, unless you shall judge it necessary to stop at Madeira, the Cape de Verd, or Canary Islands, to take in Wine for the use of their Companies; in which case you are at liberty to do so, taking care to remain there no longer than may be necessary for that purpose.

On your arrival at the Cape of Good Hope you are to refresh the Sloops Companies, and to cause the Sloops to be supplied with as much Provisions and Water as they can conveniently stow.

You are if possible to leave the Cape of Good Hope by the end of October, or the beginning of November next, and proceed to the Southward in search of some Islands said to have been lately seen by the French in the Latitude of 48°oo′ South and about the Meridian of Mauritius. - In case you find those Islands, you are to examine them thoroughly for a good Harbour, and upon discovering one make the necessary Observations to facilitate the finding it again, as a good Port, in that Situation, may hereafter prove very useful, altho' it should afford little or nothing more than shelter, wood, & water. You are not however to spend too much time in looking out for those Islands, or in the examination of them if found, but proceed to Otaheite or the Society Isles (touching at New Zealand in your way thither if you should judge it necessary and convenient) and taking care to arrive there time enough to admit of your giving the Sloops Companies the Refreshment they may stand in need of, before you prosecute the farther Object of these Instructions.

Upon your arrival at Otaheite, or the Society Isles, you are to land Omiah at such of them as he may chuse and to leave him there.

You are to distribute among the Chiefs of those Islands such part of the Presents with which you have been supplied as you shall judge proper, reserving the remainder to distribute among the Natives of the Countries you may discover in the Northern Hemisphere; and having refreshed the People belonging to the Sloops under your command, and taken on board such Wood & Water as they may respectively stand in need of, you are to leave those Islands, in the beginning of February, or sooner if you shall judge it necessary, and then proceed in as direct a Course as you can to the Coast of New Albion, endeavouring to fall in with it in the Latitude of 45°o′ North; and taking care, in your way thither, not to lose any time in search of new Lands, or to stop at any you may fall in with, unless you find it necessary to recruit your wood and water.

You are also, in your way thither, strictly enjoined not to touch upon any part of the Spanish Dominions on the Western Continent of America, unless driven thither by some unavoidable accident, in which case you are to stay no longer there than shall be absolutely necessary, and to be very careful not to give any umbrage or offence to any of the Inhabitants or Subjects of His Catholic Majesty. And if in your farther progress to the Northward, as here after directed, you find any Subjects of any European Prince or State upon any part of the Coast you may think proper to visit you are not to disturb them or give them any just cause of offence, but on the contrary to treat them with civility & friendship.

Upon your arrival on the Coast of New Albion, you are to put into the first convenient Port to recruit your Wood and Water and procure Refreshments, and then to proceed Northward along the Coast as far as the Latitude of 65°, or farther, if you are not obstructed by Lands or Ice; taking care not to lose any time in exploring Rivers or Inlets, or upon any other account, until you get into the beforementioned Latitude of 65°, where we could wish you to arrive in the Month of June next. – When you get that length, you are very carefully to search for, and to explore, such Rivers or Inlets as may appear to be of a considerable extent and pointing towards Hudsons or Baffins Bays; and, if from your own Observations, or from any information you may receive from the Natives (who, there is reason to believe, are the same Race of People, and speak the same Language, of which you are furnished with a Vocabulary, as the Esquimaux) there shall appear to be a certainty, or even a probability, of a Water Passage into the aforementioned Bays, or either of them, you are, in such case to use your utmost endeavours to pass through with one or both of the Sloops, unless you shall be of opinion that the passage may be effected with more certainty, or with greater probability, by smaller Vessels, in which case you are to set up the Frames of one or both the small Vessels with which you are provided, and when they are put together, and properly fitted, stored, & victualled, you are to dispatch one or both of them under the care of proper Officers, with a sufficient number of Petty Officers, Men, and Boats, in order to attempt the said Passage; with such Instructions for their rejoining you, if they should fail, or for their farther proceedings if they should succeed, in the attempt, as you shall judge most proper. But nevertheless if you shall find it more eligible to pursue any other measures, than those above pointed out, in order to make a discovery of the beforementioned Passage (if any such there be) you are at liberty, and we leave it to your discretion, to pursue such measures accordingly.

In case you shall be satisfied that there is no Passage through to the abovementioned Bays, sufficient for the purposes of Navigation, you are, at the proper Season of the Year, to repair to the Port of St Peter & St Paul in Kamtschatka, or wherever else you shall judge more proper, in order to refresh your People & pass the Winter; and, in the Spring of the ensuing Year 1778, to proceed from thence to the Northward as far as, in your prudence, you may think proper, in further search of a North East, or North West Passage, from the Pacific Ocean into the Atlantic Ocean, or the North Sea; and if, from your own Observation, or any information you may receive, there shall appear to be a probability, of such a Passage, you are to proceed as above directed; And, having discovered such Passage, or failed in the attempt, make the best of your way back to England by such Route as you may think best for the improvement of Geography and Navigation, repairing to Spithead with both Sloops, where they are to remain 'til further Order.

At whatever Places you may touch in the course of your Voyage, where accurate Observations of the nature hereafter mentioned have not already been made, you are, as far as your time will allow, very carefully to observe the true Situation of such Places, both in Latitude & Longitude; the Variation of the Needle; Bearings of Head lands; Height, Direction, and Course of the Tydes and Currents; Depths & Soundings of the Sea; Shoals, Rocks

&ca; and also to survey, make Charts, and take views of, such Bays, Harbours, and different parts of the Coast, and to make such Notations thereon, as may be useful either to Navigation or Commerce. You are also carefully to observe the nature of the Soil & the produce thereof; the Animals & Fowls that inhabit or frequent it; the Fishes that are to be found in the Rivers or upon the Coast, and in what plenty; and, in case there are any, peculiar to such places, to describe them as minutely, and to make as accurate drawings of them, as you can; And, if you find any Metals, Minerals, or valuable Stones, or any extraneous Fossils, you are to bring home Specimens of each, as also of the Seeds of such Trees, Shrubs, Plants, Fruits and Grains, peculiar to those Places, as you may be able to collect, and to transmit them to our Secretary, that proper examination and experiments may be made of them. – You are likewise to observe the Genius, Temper, Disposition, and Number of the Natives and Inhabitants, where you find any; and to endeavour, by all proper means to cultivate a friendship with them; making them Presents of such Trinkets as you may have on board, and they may like best; inviting them to Traffick; and shewing them every kind of Civility and Regard; but taking care nevertheless not to suffer yourself to be surprized by them, but to be always on your guard against any Accidents.

You are also with the consent of the Natives to take possession, in the Name of the King of Great Britain, of convenient Situations in such Countries as you may discover, that have not already been discovered or visited by any other European Power, and to distribute among the Inhabitants such Things as will remain as Traces and Testimonies of your having been there; But if you find the Countries so discovered are uninhabited, you are to take possession of them for His Majesty by setting up proper Marks and Inscriptions as first Discoverers & Possessors.

But for as much as in undertakings of this nature, several Emergencies may arise not to be foreseen, & therefore not particularly to be provided for by Instructions beforehand; You are, in all such Cases, to proceed, as you shall judge most advantageous to the Service on which you are employed.

You are, by all opportunities to send to our Secretary, for our information, Accounts of your Proceedings, and Copies of the Surveys and Drawings you shall have made; and upon your arrival in England, you are immediately to repair to this Office in order to lay before us a full Account of your Proceedings in the whole course of your Voyage; taking care before you leave the Sloop to demand from the Officers & Petty Officers the Log Books & Journals they may have kept, & to seal them up for our Inspection, and enjoining Them & the whole Crew, not to divulge where they have been, until they shall have permission so to do. - And you are to direct Captain Clerke to do the same with respect to the Officers, Petty Officers, and Crew of the Discovery.

If any Accident should happen to the Resolution in the course of the Voyage so as to disable her from proceeding any farther, you are, in such case, to remove yourself and her Crew into the Discovery and to prosecute your Voyage in her, her Commander being hereby strictly required to receive you on board and to obey your Orders the same in every respect as when you were actually on board the Resolution; And, in case of your inability by sickness or otherwise to carry these Instructions into execution, you are to be careful to leave them with the next Officer in command who is hereby required to execute them in the best manner he can.

Given under our hands the 6th day of July 1776.

SANDWICH
C. SPENCER
H. PALLISER

By command of their Lordships
    Php Stephens.

On first reading these Instructions, and every time since, even now while I have been copying them, my mind has dwelt on those last lines. That their Lordships should require provision to be made in the event of the Commander falling sick or worse is normal practice in the Service. Nonetheless, it cannot but have the effect of causing me to think upon it, knowing that in the more than six years I have been at sea on two very arduous voyages I have been most fortunate, not only as regards sickness, but also as regards the safety of myself and the ship, we having been many times sailing close to most dangerous shores where no ship to my knowledge has been before, and some time have been ashore where the people are unfriendly.

From what I have learned, particularly from the Russian voyages, where we are intended to go now I may expect the worst as regards weather and ice, and both coasts and possibly the people also unfriendly. As early as February, just after I had been appointed to this Command, in a letter to Mr Walker of Whitby, to whom I was first apprenticed on board the *Freelove* and who offered me command of the *Friendship* when I was only 26, I did write something to the effect that I had quit an easy retirement for a Dangerous Voyage, adding that if I were fortunate enough to get safe home it would be greatly to my advantage.

There was never any other of those I corresponded with to whom I would have written thus, he being not only understanding of the dangers of the sea, but also a most benevolent person and to me something of a second father, having given me so much help and encouragement in what I most wished to do. Not even to Mrs Cook did I ever communicate my thoughts about the Dangers, nor shall do when I send to her from the Cape if there be some suitable ship at anchor to convey my report of the Voyage thus far to the Admiralty. It is something that is between me and my Maker, this feeling that no man can for ever be so fortunate as I have been until now and that a man approaching 50 cannot but view the hazards of attempting what so many others have tried and failed without some sober thought of the trials and difficulties ahead.

But I have said enough on this subject. I feel no different in myself than when I took the *Resolution* into those cold high latitudes of the Southern Ocean and so no cause to think we shall fare worse. Pray God Chas Clerke will catch up with me in Table Bay. At 33, he is the most experienced of my officers, devoted to his work and I believe to me, and what is more he is full of spirit and a goodly sense of humour, so making light of all difficulties. I should miss him greatly were he to be prevented from joining his ship.

7
A ROB OF LEMONS

Sunday, September 29th

All the remainder of this month there has been little to remark upon, save for the birds and the fish that are always with us. Also the seams have opened up again and when it rains water pours into the cabbins and the gunroom so that there is nowhere fit to sleep, all being wet. I keep the People as active and occupied as possible, but it being very warm there is little inclination to do more than is necessary. Now it is become a little cooler as we move into the S. Atlantic. As far as we can tell we have not been nearer than perhaps 20 leagues from the coast of Brazil, but nothing certain as we had no sight of land nor any bottom by sounding. Around 8°S, in the course we take for full advantage of the Wind, the land of Brazil protrudes so far to the Eastward that the danger of falling upon it at night is always of great concern, the current being an additional hazard. During three or four days we had it setting to the Westward and then for the period of at least a day it set strong to the Northward, we being so much as 29 miles out in our reckoning.

But my greatest concern during the past weeks has been for the health of the People under my command, most of them being quite unused to giving any sort of consideration to the state of their bodies until they have become diseased. Washing in sea water is done every day, and in this the officers as well as myself set the example, for the crowded state of the ship makes hygiene somewhat a case of the horse to water, for you cannot make him drink except you do it by example. This we learned in the *Endeavour* when they refused the portable soup, but when it was served to the officers, and they at my orders showing every sign of enjoying it, the men could not get enough of it.

We have this soup served on the Banyan Days which are the meatless days and in the Navy are Mondays, Wednesdays and Fridays, either with Pease or Wheat, which is to be preferred to the oatmeal we carried in the *Endeavour*. One ounce of the Soup is required for each man on those days, it usually taking about a quarter of an hour to dissolve, and it must be stirred all the time to prevent it burning to the copper.

I also ordered before we sailed the usual Sour Krout and Malt, also Sugar in place of Oil, a Rob of Lemons and Oranges which we had previously carried and an Inspissated Juice of Wort, which there is reason to believe from experiments may also be antiscorbutic. The Rob was made at the Apothecaries Hall and we had 5 chests of oranges and five of lemons delivered to the ships. The preparation of the Inspissated juice of Wort was under the supervision of Mr Pelham and done at Mr Jacksons premises.

All this was arranged by letters from me to the Admiralty requesting that they instruct the Victualling Board accordingly. Thus far I am glad to say we have no sickness to speak of, every man being made to air his cloathes and bedding whenever possible and the ship aired throughout by ventilation as well as being cleansed by smoking pots set down in all the lower parts.

This is a rigorous routine and one that requires enforcement by firm discipline. Such discipline is more readily borne on the passage through the Atlantic Ocean both going out and returning since the men are fresh for the one and eager for home on the other. In the Pacific it is another matter, for there is always the distraction of the islands.

The women are pleasing and all seem of the loosest morals so that it is hard to keep our Peoples hands off anything in the ship that can be traded for that which they most want. At the same time, we have the advantage of fresh food and an abundance of fruit and vegetables, something we never have in the Atlantic, not being able to call at any place and having to rely only on what we have in the ship. Thus it is on this passage that we most benefit of the Soup, Sour Krout and other items which have been specially prepared. It is to this, and the vegetables I purchased fresh before sailing into the heat and calms of Equatorial waters, particularly I believe the onions, that is the cause of the good health we enjoy. I am not speaking here of scurvy, which is a disease more common to the Pacific than to the Atlantic, though it is my strong opinion that the hygiene I do normally practice, and the fruits, roots and other fresh plants that I gather ashore at every opportunity and feed to the men is the cause of my being so free of this scourge.

I will have more to say of this later when I can describe the plants I shall bring off to the ship. There is always something to be found even in the bleakest places and it was Mr Banks and also Dr Solander with their knowledge of Botany that enabled me that first voyage to find everywhere something edible. Even when we were in the Le Maire Strait close by Cape Horn we found wild Sellery and scurvy grass and a sort of Cranberry but larger and the fruit of a bush which was very palatable with the shell fish that we prised from the rocks.

8

THE GREAT CABBIN

Sunday, October 6th

We are now far enough south to fall in with birds of colder waters and today we have seen albatrosses for the first time, Pintadoes and other Petrels, also 3 Penguins for which reason we sounded, but no bottom on a line of 150 fathoms. During this time I have given much thought and some study to the charts and maps of North America, something I could not do too openly and so had to see to it that the Cabbin was clear or at least the others so occupied that they would not take note of the work I was engaged upon.

I remember when the great Cabbin of the *Endeavour* was crowded with Banks, Solander and Spöring, who was their assistant, all busy studying and naming fish, birds, flowers and plants, and 2 artists, Parkinson and Buchan, engaged from morning to night drawing everything most exactly, so that often I had no place for my charts nor any room to do the work for which I had been commissioned. Now there is nobody on board to study specimens and only Mr Webber, who has been engaged as artist by the Admiralty at 100 guineas a year to make drawings and paintings, and those only of the places we shall visit.

So it is very quiet here in the cabbin in comparison to what it has been previously, for even on my late voyage I had among the supernumaries the Forsters and 2 draughts-men who had been with Mr Banks on the expedition he made to Iceland. And there were always their servants in and out. For this voyage there is not even an Astronomer with me, Mr Bayly being posted into the *Discovery* for the better use of the instruments on board that ship. As a result I have quiet in the cabbin for my writing, but less time, there being a great deal of work for me to do in the care and setting up of all the varied astronomical and other Instruments and the observations to make, or otherwise to see to it that my officers do make them accurately.

I must confess, though I have learned to be solitary, and perhaps it is partly in my nature to be so or else have become so by habit, I do not entirely relish it. Thinking back to those times in the *Endeavour*, I find I enjoyed the constant activity, the conversation and the excitement of new botanical discoveries and now miss it. Always I seemed to be learning something new. But not now, for there is nobody on board to tell me anything I do not already know, excepting possibly Mr Anderson. Mr Webber is a very quick artist and likes to draw birds as well as landscapes, but he is not very interested in the creatures we bring up from the sea in our net and so has little to do on this part of the voyage, there being few birds until now and no sight of land since we cleared the Cape Verdes.

Tuesday, October 8th

Today a Noddy was taken from our rigging, being birds that are very easily captured. Mr Webber is drawing it now and I have myself noted its arrival in my Journal, also the belief that they never fly far from land. This occasions us some concern since we are 100 leagues* at the very least from Goughs island, which is a very precipitous and dangerous place being a volcano lifted up out of the sea and quite solitary in the great waters of this ocean. South of our present latitude being little frequented, there may be more islands than we know of.

* A league at sea is the equivalent of 3·18 nautical miles.

One of the difficulties always to be faced in my voyages is the lack of any constant degree of accuracy among sailors in the positioning of islands and coasts, they not having the benefit of the sort of instruments of navigation which I have on board, nor often the ability nor even the inclination to make exact observations of latitude and longitude. As for the mapmakers, I never can place absolute reliance on the results of their labours, excepting those charts of waters and ports that I know to have been properly surveyed. It seems that in their urgency to come out with a new Atlas or Map ahead of their rivals, they readily take supposition for observation and will draw in almost anything on the merest hearsay.

In regard to my Instructions, the maps I have most studied on the voyage thus far have been those of Müller* and Jacob von Stählin. The former is very open and honest in that he admits he has done no more than connect together by points according to probability the coasts that have been sighted. Both show the strait that Capt Behring claims to have sailed through reaching so far north as 67°18′ when he turned back, still having no sight of the shore. Both show the track of his ship the St Gabriel, the latter I think the more accurately. His later expedition with two ships did not progress so far north, but on this occasion both he and Chirikov separately did sight the N. American coast.

The other tracks shown on these maps are of Lt Sindos voyage in 1764-8 when he discovered and charted the Archipelago that is WSW from the coast of N. America, and the same is drawn on the Stählin map, the positioning of the islands of the Archipelago being in more detail, but a considerable difference in numbers, shape and position.

* Gerhard Friedrich Müller, official Russian historian.

PART THREE

The Cape
to New Zealand

9

Sunday, October 27th, 1776

We had sight of the Cape of Good Hope on the 17th, but did not anchor in Table Bay till a little after noon the following day, the wind blowing fresh the evening we arrived off Penguin Island. The *Discovery* is not yet arrived, the ships in the Bay being 2 French and a small Dutchman.

As soon as we were securely anchored in 4 fathoms, the Church bearing SW¼S, and had received the usual visit from the Master attendant and the Surgeon, I sent an officer to wait upon the Governor Baron Plettenburg, who had been most courteous to me on my previous voyage. On his return we saluted the Garrison with 13 guns, the like being returned. Afterwards, I went on shore with some of my officers and waited upon the Governor, his Second, the Fiscal and Major Prehn who commands the troops. All received me with the greatest respect and civility, promising every assistance.

I should I suppose feel flatered and indeed surprised that my name and what I have done should be so widely known and so much acclaimed. And yet strange to say I am not, having now become used to it in a city so much bigger than Cape Town. I did not comment on this to the Governor, but 3 days before we came in here a French Indiaman parted her cable and drove ashore and the inhabitants far from helping plundered both Ship and Cargo. Such action is a disgrace to any civilised community and the Dutch it seems excuse themselves from being guilty of any crime by blaming the Captain for not applying for a guard in time, but when he did apply there were obstacles put in his way and on the guard finally arriving matters were not mended but worse

73

than before. In short, Cape Town is a place where the Dutch regard all Strangers as fair game and as much to be got from them as is possible, whether the means are justified or not.

Having been told of these events by the French, I am now very careful, and constantly enjoin my officers to be on their guard, the which somewhat detracts from the civility and honour I receive officially. I had leave to set up our observatory wherever I wished, but the most suitable place was one where the Militia was exercising, so it was not until the 22nd that we had the tents for sailmakers and coopers ashore and all else we required, and it was the following day before we began to observe equal altitude of the Sun for ascertaining the rate of the Watch. Weather permitting this we shall continue every day until the time for our departure, the rate of the Timekeeper being of the utmost importance for the accurate determination of the position of the islands in the South Pacific that Kerguelen sighted and others nearer at hand that the French Lt Crozet spoke to me about when I met with him here at the Cape in March 1775.

Yesterday one of the French ships sailed for France and by her I sent a brief report to the Admiralty, also letters, my own and others. Whether they reach home safe I do not know, but am assured they will, the which I hope very much as I do not know when, nor by what means, Mrs Cook may hear from me again. The best hope is perhaps from some Russian port, and that a long way from England and not very reliable, since the Instructions I have for the Pacific and the route that I shall take makes the falling in with some other ship a most unlikely possibility.

On the 22nd I dined at the Garrison with the Governor and had 3 royal salutes of 21 guns and many Toasts.

IO

THE DISCOVERY AT LAST

Thursday, November 28th

My anger and contempt for the Dutch is at times so great that I find myself almost shaking with it, they having behaved very perfidiously for all their protestations of respect.

But first I must state what has happened in the near 5 weeks since I last wrote anything here. I was ashore, and not in the ship, the better to overlook the observations and arrange all the stores we required. Apart from the arrival of the *Hampshire* Indiaman from Bencoolen, which saluted us with 13 guns, our replying with 11, no great event occurred until the evening of October 31st when it came on to blow exceeding hard from SE. This gale continued for 3 days and for that period all communication between ship and shore was impossible. The *Resolution* was in fact the only ship in the Road that did not drag her anchors. Ashore we had our tents and observatory blown to pieces and the Astronomical Quadrant was near ruined.

On November 6th the *Hampshire* sailed for England and I sent home in her the armourer Wm Hunt for trial, he being discovered making false coins. I handed him over to the Governor, since it was most like he made the money on shore and not on the ship. But the Governor would have none of it, so I had him disciplined and put on board the *Hampshire*, it not being my wish to have him cause any further trouble on the voyage and this being a civil matter. There were 3 men sick at the time which I would also have sent home, but that 2 of them, a carpenters mate and a quartermaster, I could ill spare and Mr Anderson had hopes of all three recovering.

Then on the 10th the *Discovery* came in. The sight of her that morning coming out of the rain and fog to anchor in the Road was a matter of great satisfaction and relief. It is never sensible, or at least should not be considered so, to take the risks necessary for the proper survey of unknown coasts but that there are two ships so that in the event one go upon a reef or be set ashore there is another to save the men in her. This was the situation on my first voyage, the *Endeavour* being alone in unknown waters for more than 3 years and when we went upon the reef off the north east coast of New Holland there was no other ship to help us and only good fortune and our own efforts saved us and brought the ship safe to an anchorage in the river further north along the coast.

My relief at the *Discovery*s arrival was the greater when Capt Clerke himself reported to me. He had sailed from Plymouth on August 1st, having got himself clear of the Israelites and out of that wretched prison into which he had been committed. He said he would have arrived a week earlier but that in a calm he was almost set down on Penguin Island, and having anchored was then forced by a gale of wind to fetch the anchor, a matter that took near on 2 hours such was the confusion on board. He had rode out the gale with North Passage open under his lee and had had good holding there.

He told it all so humorously that I felt the necessity of informing him what had happened to the Frenchman that was driven ashore and also that my need of a consort on the voyage was such that he must at all times exercise the greatest care for his Ship. In fact, I had not expected him earlier, for I had taken the most Westerly route down the Atlantic, sailing closer than heretofor to the coast of Brazil, thereby missing the Equatorial calms and having a reasonable fast passage.

The *Discovery* was also in want of caulking and this work being now finished on board of the *Resolution* I sent all my caulkers to work on his ship. I also gave him every other assistance to get on board his Water and the provisions I had already ordered. The bread I had ordered baked for the *Discovery* was not yet done for want of flour they said, but the truth of the matter was that the bakers had not thought she would arrive. This sort of pessimism is something that I have constantly to fight against. It seems to be in the nature of men that their spirits will not be lifted but the Commander is constantly letting it be known by the Rumours that are ever running between decks that he is sanguine of everything, including the outcome of the whole voyage.

I I

OF SHEEP AND GOATS
AND THE WATCH

Now I must relate what has caused the anger to which I referred earlier. The night preceding the 14th some felons put dogs into the pen ashore where we kept our sheep, which numbered 16. They killed 4 sheep and the rest were broke out of the pen. Six were found next day, but 1 ram and 2 of the finest ewes were amongst those that were missing. The Governor being absent, I saw his Second and also the Fiscal, but their promise of action for the recovery of the animals was greater than their endeavours, so that I am not by any means convinced that some of the first people in Cape Town did not have a hand in the business.

This is a place where I am told that a slave with all his cunning and knowledge of the Country cannot escape from the Police, yet my sheep had no difficulty in evading the fiscals. I had recourse then to the scoundrels of the town, having been recommended to them by others who had suffered a like experience. These are men who for a suitable recompense will cut their Masters throat, burn his house over him and bury his body and all his family in the ashes. Through them I recovered all but the 2 ewes. One of the rams being so badly injured it was doubtful he would live, Mr Hemmy, the Second Governor, offered to make good the loss, but I did not accept, satisfied that the Cape ram I had purchased would serve as well.

After this disaster I did not let those sheep that remained stay long on shore, but got them and the other cattle on board. And to the animals we already had I have now added 2 young bulls, 2 heifers, 2 young stone horses, 2 mares, 2 rams, some ewes and goats, also rabbits and poultry. They are intended for New Zealand and the islands of the Pacific, indeed anywhere where posterity may benefit from their being left.

The *Discovery* is now caulked and has got on board all her provisions and water. We have done the same, including everything I could think we might want in the next two years, for I did not know when we should come to a place where we could supply ourselves so well. This has been one of my chiefest concerns, for we sail in a day or two and once we lose sight of the Cape there is no turning back, and ahead nothing of certainty save the lands and islands I have already visited.

Much of my time has been taken up with the observations,

but on the 23rd we got the Clock and the observatory on board having done I think all that we could to establish the rate of the Watch. I will not repeat the details of our calculations, which are all set down in the Book and also the Journal, only the results, which after 15 days of observations, taking the mean of them, we find the error of the Watch in longitude no more than 8′25″. Thus we had reason to conclude she had gone well all the way from England and the longitude that resulted nearer the truth than any other has given me. This is of great importance for the determining of currents, as off the coast of Brazil where from 2°N 25°W to 13°S 30°W in the space of 4 days we had an error in the Ships reckoning of 115 miles SWbyW the cause of which I now take to be a strong current setting in that direction.

Mr Anderson is now returned some days from a Wagon journey he made to Stellenbosh and other places in the vicinity of Cape Town. He is very full of all that he has seen, as are those that went with him, in particular the vineyards and orchards and the neatness of the farmhouses. His seeking for plants and insects was not well rewarded, but at Stellenbosh he and the others were entertained at a house that had a wine cellar and were received there with music, a band playing while they dined. Returning on the 20th much jolted by the Wagon he had all the insects he could wish, being much devoured by what he thinks may have been sandflies, the same we suffered from so badly last voyage when lying a month and more at Mr Pickersgills Harbour in Dusky Bay.*

* Dusky Bay is in South Island, New Zealand, a dismal place with a very high rainfall where I was plagued by sandflies on my visit there in 1970.

12

THE FIRST OBJECTIVE

Friday, December 6th

We are now at sea again and I back in the cabbin, having finally repaired on board the *Resolution* on the morning of November 30th after giving Capt Clerke a copy of my Instructions for the immediate voyage. I also gave him orders how to proceed in the event we become separated, the which I think less likely than happened with Capt Furneaux on the previous voyage, for though the *Discovery* is smaller and will sail slower, Chas Clerke is a much more tenacious man and understands my thoughts very well.

We had no wind on going aboard, but about 5 in the afternoon a breeze sprung up from the SE and we stood out of the Bay, saluting the Garrison with our guns and they replying. By 9 it was calm again and we anchored between Penguin Island and the East shore where we lay till 3 in the morning, when we weighed again with a light breeze at S. The wind remained somewhat light so that it was not until December 3rd we got finally clear of the land with a fresh gale at WNW.

There is always a bad sea in the vicinity of the Cape and this occasion was no exception, the sea breaking with great violence over the ship and entering by way of the hatches so that all were very wet. But at the least the wind set us well on our way towards the first of the islands I wished to examine, which are those discovered by the French Capts Morion and Crozet in January 1772.

The fine start we had was something marred yesterday the 5th when we had the Mizzen Topmast brought down by a heavy squal of wind. The loss was not great, for it had given us cause for concern previously being a bad stick and we had another with which we soon replaced it.

Today we sailed through a number of small patches of sea that have a reddish colour. This was in the evening, our position being 39°14′S, 23°56′E, and when we brought up water in a bucket it had in it small creatures the size of a louse, which examined with the Microscope were like a kind of shrimp of a very red colour. These patches of red lie in streaks over the waves, even colouring the white as they break. I think them to be the same that Mr Banks and Dr Solander named when the *Endeavour* sailed through similar red patches coloured by minute crawfish in the South Atlantic. There was some talk then that they are the food of whales and porpoises for these animals were present in some numbers at the time.

Tuesday, December 17th

Though in the Southern Ocean, the weather we now have is such as we would expect in the north of England at midwinter, very cold and Thick with strong gales between north and west. Every man now has served out to him a good stout Magelline* Jacket and a pair of Fearnought Trowsers providing him with some protection against the weather, which though very indifferent, is not yet near as bad as we suffered on my late voyage when we sailed as far south as 71°10′S among islands of ice, our rigging froze and watering the ship by sending boats to cut blocks of ice. Our clothing was ill-suited to those extremes of cold and I had a fire lit in the great cabbin.

Here we are no further south than Lat 48°25′S and it is

* Presumably the jackets were named after Magellan, the Portuguese navigator, who entered and named the Pacific in 1520.

the Fog that is my chiefest concern. Not a day passes but that we lose sight of the *Discovery* and it is only with the greatest difficulty and the most constant vigilance on the part of both that we are kept together. Conditions are most miserable for everyone, the ship leaking as before, all wet below and water getting in to the sail room, so that the sails must be brought out on deck to dry on every opportunity.

On the 12th we sighted the islands that Capt Crozet spoke to me of, there being two of them, the one larger than the other and very barren, the tops covered in snow. They were in Lat.46°53′S, Long.37°46′E. To distinguish them, they being unnamed on the French chart, I named the smaller Prince Edward Island, and that to the Southward, we passing between them, Morion and Crozet Island. Now my course is East for we are on the latitude given me by Capt Bourdat for the island Monsieur de Kerguelen named Rendezvous, though I do not know why since there can be no rendezvous here but for the fowls of the air. I am sailing a zig-zag course with the lookouts instructed to watch both ahead for the island and astern for the *Discovery* which we have again lost sight of, though continually hauling our wind to allow her to catch up with us.

It will soon be Christmas and a time when men who are at sea get drunk if they can, the reason I think being to dull the ache of thinking about their homes and families. When I consider how few Christmas days I have spent with Mrs Cook and our family it is not something I wish my mind to dwell upon and so shall keep occupied. There will be no great difficulty in this for we are searching blind for an island I sometimes believe does not exist. But this is only when the eyes get tired with staring into the white wall of vapour. I have the position, and I know it does exist, but reason is not easily sustained when for many hours at a time I am not able to see twice the length of the ship and we are firing a gun every hour so that we keep company with Capt Clerke by sound alone.

Any fears I have that we may suddenly find ourselves upon a reef I keep only to myself. Did the men, or even the officers, see how troubled I am, knowing there is a mass of sheer rock somewhere ahead of us, it would be instantly conveyed through the ship and everyone then afraid for their lives. Fear is something that is dreadful to contemplate on board of a ship, it being as contagious as the plague and equally dangerous since men are not then amenable to discipline, the marines equally so, with the result that there is nothing to prevent mutiny. Already the officers are talking among themselves. They do not see the purpose of exploring and charting these islands, not being privy to my Instructions and wondering all the time what the Plan of the Voyage really is.

13
CHRISTMAS, 1776

Friday, December 27th

Continuing to steer an Eastward course, the fog cleared somewhat and we saw land bearing SSE. This was at six on the morning of the 24th and the sight of it was the greatest relief, our navigation these past few days having been both tedious and dangerous, but as this is what I fear we shall have a great deal of in the northernmost limits of the Pacific I have considered it of considerable benefit to everybody, most particularly the officers.

Approaching the land we found it to be an island of some considerable height and about 3 leagues in circuit. There was another of the same magnitude to the east of it with smaller ones between, and with the fog breaking up we thought we could see land over the smaller islands. I had thought to steer between the two chief islands, but on approaching found it to be dangerous with the fog still about, they being to leeward and no way to run the ship off if we found no passage through. The wind was right on and a prodigious sea running that broke on all the shores of the island in a frightful surf. So I hauled off to wait for the fog to clear fearing we should become entangled among those islands in thick fog. Even so, we did but just weather the second of the larger islands.

By 11 o'clock, the weather clearing, we tacked and stood in for the land. At noon we had pretty clear observation, so that we were able to determine the position of the northernmost island as Lat.48°29'S Long.68°40'E. We were past the point of it which I named Blighs Cap by 3 o'clock in a fresh westerly gale and had land in sight, the same that we had seen above the small islands that morning. The left extreme of it appeared to be the headland Kerguelen had named Cape St. Louis. It terminated in a perpendicular rock of some considerable height, and there appearing to be an inlet halfway along the coast, we stood directly for it, but finding it to be no more than a bend in the coast I bore up for the Cape and having rounded it, found the coast much indented.

I was seeking a harbour here for the night, but after making one board it fell calm, so I anchored off the first inlet in 45 fathoms black sand and sent Mr Bligh in to sound. He reported good anchorage, in every part a great plenty of fresh water and numerous seals, penguins and all manner of birds, but no wood. The *Discovery* was by then caught up. It being almost dark, both ships remained anchored in the entrance during the night, we observing that the flood ran at least 2 knots from SE.

And so on the morning of Christmas Day, with a gentle breeze at west, we worked to within a quarter of a mile of a dark sand beach, where we let go in 8 fathoms. I called this Christmas Harbour, though Capt Clerke had a poor day of it, he being very near set ashore on the southern point, his anchor starting before he could shorten cable and they having to sail with it still down, so breaking one of its palms. This appears to have been due to a fault in the metal.

It was very unlike other Christmases I have spent at sea, for we had no chance to celebrate, it being very urgent that we refill the water casks in case some gale of wind forced us to leave in haste. Water was very plentiful, as were the birds, and the seals being quite without fear we killed the number we required for the rendering down of their blubber into oil for our lamps. There were no trees nor a single shrub, and though the sides of the hills were a bright green, it was not grass, but a plant that grows very plentiful in these islands.

And after I had set all to work, I climbed a ridge of rocks that was piled up in stairs like the seats in a Roman amphitheatre. But having got to the top of it, saw nothing of the islands, the fog coming down so thick I had to call out for guidance otherwise I would have been lost. We had one of the seine nets the Admiralty had procured for me hauled across the entrance but with little success, so that we had to rely on birds for our fresh provisions and these we got in plenty.

The activities of both ships was so great that day that I doubt whether any man really believed it to be Christmas Day. And the next day was no better, the filling of the casks with water having to be completed and all to be rowed back and forth between beach and ship, also grass for the cattle to be conveyed in the same manner after being cut from small sheltered areas at the head of the inlet where it did grow. All this work, and the killing of the seals and birds, was much hampered by rain, which was so heavy that the bare rock of the hillside was a sheet of water and every gully a raging torrent.

Thus it was not until today, the 27th, when I was fully satisfied that we were assured of a sufficiency of fresh provisions and water, that I was able to order the proper celebration of Christmas. Many of the men took this as an opportunity of exploring ashore and it was some relief in the evening to have a report that all were safe back on board and no-one lost. One of them brought a bottle to me he had found hanging to a rock on the north side of the inlet. It had a piece of parchment in it on which had been written:

> *Ludovico XV galliarum*
> *rege.et d. de Boynes*
> *regi a Secretis ad res*
> *maritimas annis 1772 et*
> *1773*

thus making it clear that Kerguelen had used this same harbour when he first landed on this island February 13th 1772, which date is noted on the French chart of the Southern Hemisphere. I did thereupon cause to be written on the other side of the parchment:

> *Naves Resolution*
> *& Discovery*
> *de Rege Magnæ Brittaniæ*
> *Decembris 1776*

and returned it to the bottle with a silver 2 penny piece of

1772, which was Maundy money, two of which I had of Mr Kings chaplain, my friend Dr Kaye. I had the mouth of the bottle covered with a leaden cap and tomorrow will erect a cairn in some prominent position at the head of the harbour as I have done at various places on my voyages.

14

PLANTS AND SEAWEED

Wednesday, January 1st, 1777

Yesterday morning I was much relieved to have several observations of both Sun and Moon, something we had not been able to accomplish for some time due to fog and cloud. These showing no material error in the Timekeeper I am confident that we shall make our landfall correctly in Van Diemens Land*, which is where I am now headed, having left Kerguelens islands on December 30th, the last of which I named the Island of Desolation it being even more bleak and sterile than the main land.

It is no way surprising that the first discoverers of it imagined this could be a cape of the Southern Continent, but we had a big swell from the south west, clear indication to anyone encountering it that there could be no mass of land in that direction. And Capt Furneauxs log, which I have with me, shows that after he had separated from me he sailed to the south of it in such clear weather that he was able to establish his position by observation.

In the six days we were in the islands some considerable part of my time was taken up with examining such plants

* At that time the name for Tasmania.

as there are, and also the numerous birds and the nature of
the rocks, and in writing all this into my Journal. This is a
labour I have come to regard as of equal, if not greater
import than the preparation of accurate charts of the coastline, which had been my chiefest concern on previous voyages. The work that I did the year I was ashore in England
preparing my Journal for press, the demand of the Publick
for entertainment and information, and indeed the attitude
of everyone I talked with, their Lordships and fellow members of the Royal Society included, has convinced me that,
if I am to be suitably rewarded for all my endeavours, I
have to use my time in the lands and islands I visit to produce a different sort of Journal, one that will appeal to the
imagination and be ready for press immediately upon my
return.

I shall be more than 50 years of age by the time I return.
This will almost certainly be my last long voyage of discovery, my last and greatest opportunity to make my name
and what I have done known to the larger world of the
Publick. I have nobody, except my surgeon Mr Anderson,
who is in any way understanding of natural history and must
rely upon my own powers of observation, remembering
what I learned from Mr Banks, Dr Solander and Mr Spöring,
in the *Endeavour*, and to a lesser degree from the Forsters
on my last voyage.

It is surprising that, even on these very barren islands, I
was able to find plants that could be eaten to the benefit
of everybody. Besides the sort of saxifrage, which made the
hillsides so green they might have been covered by verdure,
there was in the boggy declivities a plant growing quite
plentifully about 2 feet high and not unlike a cabbage going
to seed. It had 3 or 4 stalks growing separately from the root
with long cylindrical heads composed of small flowers. It
had the same appearance and the watery acrid taste of anti-

scorbutic plants, though being different it is to be regarded as peculiar to these islands. We all of us ate it raw, I firmly believe to the great advantage of our health, but when boild it had a rank flavour, though some of the men seemed not to notice this and thought it good whether boild or raw. Unfortunately, the seeds were not yet ripened, so that I could not take any with me to experiment with when Mr Nelson* the gardener is able to arrange the cultivation of kitchen gardens ashore for the benefit of the peoples we visit, this being I believe as important as the leaving ashore of our livestock in suitable places.

There was also 2 other plants growing by brooks or in bogs, one like cress but very fiery to the taste, the other quite mild. We did eat these as a sallad, and some also ate it boild when it too had a rank hot taste to use Mr Gores words who thinks it a good antiscorbutic. Altogether there are not above 18 different plants, including various sorts of moss, a very pretty lichen and the grass we cut for our cattle.

I could wish that I knew more about the sea plants, and the uses to which they may be put. In particular, the weed that is like some form of kelp that we ran into after leaving Christmas Harbour, the same that we had encountered in the Le Maire Strait seven years ago and which Mr Banks identified as *Fucus giganteus*. Its stems are no thicker than a man's thumb, yet it grows to a most prodigious length, and not perpendicular to the sea bed, but at an acute angle.

We were steering SEbyS along the coast from the foreland I had called Hows after Admiral Lord How when we passed through a mass of rocks and islets, and afterward the sea ahead of us became chequered with large beds of this weed. The situation was hazardous, knowing the weed to be fixed

* David Nelson, a gardener at Kew loaned by Banks, sailed in the *Discovery*, acting also as servant to William Bailey, the astronomer.

to the bottom and always to grow upon rocky shelves, and the sea at the time being calm as a mill pond with no surge to reveal the hidden reefs. We steered through winding channels between the weed and after running in this manner for upward of an hour we chanced on a lurking rock just level with the surface of the sea right in the centre of one of these large beds of weed.

We were then about 8 miles off Hows Foreland across the mouth of a large bay with low islands and rocks in the entrance of it and more of these beds of weeds. After continuing our course half an hour I resolved it was so dangerous I hauld off to the Eastward to get into the open sea away from the land. But we were then into more weed and with the weather thickening, and we running over the edges of shoals with 10 to 20 fathoms depth, the moment we were over no bottom at 50 fathoms, I ordered Capt Clerke to lead in for the shore in search of an anchorage, the *Discovery* drawing less than ourselves. We were both of us anchored safely by 5 o'clock, just before it came on to blow so hard we had to strike our Topgallant yards.

I believe this weed to grow 60 fathoms* and more in length. Certainly we had no bottom on a line of 24 fathoms sailing through it and as I have indicated it grows at an acute angle to the bottom. Whether we shall encounter it with the same length of growth in the North Pacific as we do here I do not know, but encounter it I am sure we shall.

Sailing the ships along the dangerous coasts of these islands is a reminder to me of the hazards that lie ahead. It has had its uses, apart from observations and charting, for it has been a very practical warning to the officers, and I think to the men also, of the need of a constant watch and the readiness to handle the ships with the greatest alacrity.

* A fathom being 6 feet this gives the kelp a stem length of 360 feet and more.

15
ON BOARD OF A CAT

I have always referred to the ease of handling these ships. There is none built anywhere that I have found so entirely suited to the purpose of surveying uncharted and dangerous coasts. This I have proved, never at any time wanting a better. Slowness of sailing is no disadvantage in this work. What is important is to be able to stop the ship dead and turn her in her own length, the which they do very readily. I am told they look clumsy, but that is only to those who have not sailed in them or who do not understand what is required of the work on which I have been so constantly engaged these last 8 years.

Something that was often asked of me ashore, particularly by the Ladies, was how big were the ships and what it was like to live so long on board of them. This was never an easy question to answer, for when I said the *Resolution* was of 462 tons berthen, it was immediately apparent that the tonnage gave them no idea of the size and all had to be converted into feet. Thus we live on board of a ship that is almost 112 feet long at the level of the lower deck, 35½ feet at the greatest breadth and a little over 13 feet deep in the hold. The *Adventure*, my consort on the previous voyage, was of 340 tons, but in the *Discovery* Capt Clerke has one of the smaller colliers built at Whitby, the tonnage being only 298, the lower deck length 91 feet, breadth 27½ feet, depth 11½ feet. When I arranged for their purchase the cost of the *Resolution* was £4151 and the *Discovery* £1865, but this was before the alterations necessary to fit them out for the purpose for which the Admiralty required them which was considerable.

They are, as can be seen from the measurements, very full-bodied and roomy with good Cargo space, the which is very necessary for we have of some provisions a full 3 years supply and are carrying a great number of livestock. So little room have we on board that Omai was forced to give up his cabbin to 2 horses when they were brought on board from the Cape, the which he seemed quite happy to do. But if we are more crowded than in some of His Majestys ships of war, at least we have the advantage of going on shore in various places and there is no threat to life and limb from the chances of battle. The leaking of the upper works has been a greater discomfort than the numbers that have to find room to lie in a small ship. At sea this is no great problem since watches greatly reduce the difficulty of accommodating the People below decks. And when we are at anchor in warmer waters, which we shall be after leaving New Zealand, the deck becomes a better place to sleep than below.

The question of what it is like to live on board these ships thus has no simple answer, but I can say that in all the years I have now been voyaging in them trouble with the men has never arisen on account of the confined space. There is most times plenty of work to keep them occupied, and when the ship makes no demands many follow the lead of myself and my officers and are busy writing their journals. Only when we are becalmed for too long a period do I have any reason to be concerned. And I know from all the reports of voyages that I have read that this is something that has been the bane of all commanders, most particularly in Equatorial regions where added to the heat is the dreadful presence of disease. This I am glad to say is something of which I have a different experience and I pray it will be so again on this voyage, which is why at every opportunity I bring on board fresh plants and roots and shall continue so to do.

16

VAN DIEMENS LAND

Sunday, February 9th

We have now traversed 105° of longitude in the 42 days since leaving the Island of Desolation, which is not much more than 100 miles each day though always carrying as much sail as possible. This we must do, for when we reach New Zealand, which we may do tomorrow if our observations are correct, we then have the whole Pacific Ocean ahead of us. From New Zealand to the Straits that Capt Behring discovered, and the sea passage across the N of America to the Atlantick ocean if any such Passage exist, it is 107° of latitude, a distance of some 2500 leagues in a straight line. But we cannot sail in a straight line, having to take advantage of the winds that prevail in the various latitudes. And we cannot sail continuously, there being our casks to fill with water, something that is very necessary for our survival, most particularly in the heat of the lower latitudes. Thus we must call at various islands, and discover others where there is water, in addition to taking the fullest advantage of any rain storms and squals that are common in the central Pacific. We have with us on this voyage a still for making fresh water from sea water, the which we were not able to try until we reached Van Diemens Land, having found no wood in those barren Kerguelen islands.

The delays we had at Deptford before we left on this voyage are now pressing upon me. The fitting out of the *Resolution* for a voyage to remote parts was ordered as long ago as 13th September 1775, but she was not ready to receive men until early January last year and in fact did not take in men till 10th February. For this, and the fact that she did not go down to the Norse until mid-June, I am in part to blame in that I was greatly occupied at home with my Journal and so not present as I was prior to the two previous voyages to give that sense of urgency to the preparations that drives men to their fullest endeavour.

Now we shall be hard put to make those distant Straits before the short northern summer is over and ice begins to form again. This I know from my own experience in the St Lawrence to happen very early, probably in late September or early October. After I was in the St Lawrence I was 3 years Master of the Flagship of the American Squadron surveying the Nova Scotia and Newfoundland coasts, and when the late War* ended in 1763 I was given my own command, the schooner *Grenville*, and was a further 5 years surveying those foggy Eastern Coasts of North America. I am thus very well acquainted with the harshness and length of the Winter and do not think from what I have been able to read that the conditions on the western coasts of that cold continent will greatly differ from those I experienced all those years on the eastern side.

It is thus very necessary that we do press on with the utmost dispatch, hastening our preparations in Queen Charlottes Sound and thereafter taking every advantage of the wind to make to the northward as rapidly as possible, I having no commitment in my Instructions other than to return Omai to his native islands and to make what new discoveries I can in our passage northwards. It was this necessity to carry all Sail possible that caused the loss of our Fore Topmast which carried away the Main Topgallant Mast with it at 4 o'clock in the morning of Sunday 19th January in a sudden

* This was the war that later became known as the Seven Years' War.

squall of wind. This delayed us most of the day, clearing the wreckage and fitting another Topmast. The Topgallant we could not replace as we had neither spare nor any suitable spar on board.

During these days when we were sailing without sight of land on the voyage to Van Diemens Land, and also since, I have spent much time studying the two maps of the Russian and North American coasts and endeavouring in every way to prepare myself for the great opportunity that lies ahead. By constant study, and in the light of my experience, it does seem possible for me to form in my mind some semblance of a visual impression of what we may expect. This is something I have always been able to do, so converting the map into an imagined reality of sea and rock and weather. But though this has the salutory effect of preparing myself for the physical eventualities, I have found that the picture I have formed of it in my mind is never so accurate that the reality of it does not take me somewhat by surprise, the unexpected resolving itself when least expected so that once we are in unknown waters, feeling our way along an unknown coast, I know there will be no rest for me. Nevertheless, I have these past weeks, and will continue to do whatever I can to prepare myself, knowing that to arrive off those northern coasts too late in the year is to put myself, my People and my ships in the greatest hazard.

This is why, when we arrived at Van Diemens Land, I went straight into Adventure Bay, where I had previously anchored in March 1773, doing only what had to be done and not making any further survey of the coast. The officers, all except Capt Clerke who knew very well the urgency of our sailing, could not understand why, having spent time exploring the Crozet and Kerguelen islands, I did not take this opportunity to map the coast of Van Diemens

Land.* I could not tell them I was committed to the exploration of the former, but had no such orders for the latter. In any event, the time we were in those islands there was little wind with the fog so that it was no great loss of our progress Eastward.

We sighted the coast of Van Diemens Land bearing N½W at 3 a.m. on 24th January, but then lost the westerly wind and had in its place variable light airs and calm so that it was not until Sunday 26th at 4 in the afternoon that we anchored in Adventure Bay in 12 feet on a bottom of sand and owse. There was little grass, which was our greatest need for the cattle, and that not good, but an abundance of wood and water. The following day, whilst engaged on these duties, I posted a guard of Marines, having sighted smoke inland though no sign of the inhabitants, but Capt Clerkes Marines stole some liquor and got so exceeding drunk they were put into the boat like corpses. They received a dozen lashes each. That evening we had a great many fish in the seine net at the head of the bay, but an Elephant Fish broke it as it was being drawn ashore so that the catch was not so great and the Elephant Fish not much better eating than shark.

Mr Bayly had got the Observatory tent and all his instruments of navigation ashore, but it being cloudy all day he was not able to obtain observations, and in the evening I ordered him to get the whole on board again so that we were ready for sea. But the next morning there being no wind we continued loading wood and water and I sent the Carpenter

* If he had done so Cook would have discovered it was an island, something which was not entered on any map of New Holland (Australia) until after Bass had deduced the existence of the Strait named after him and a year later had proved that his deduction was correct by sailing through it with Flinders in the *Reliance* in December 1798.

ashore to cut spars, also Mr Roberts, one of the Mates, to survey the Bay. In the afternoon we had our first sight of the inhabitants, 8 men and a boy coming to us out of the woods, unarmed and with the greatest confidence. They were quite naked, black with what I finally agreed with Mr King was hair as woolly as the natives of New Guinea. They are quite different from those I had met with previously in the north of New Holland, and not at all like the miserable desert people Dampier describes having seen on the western coast. One of them had a stick with him which he used as a throwing weapon, but he did not seem very good at it when a mark was set up at 20 yards and Omai told him to throw at it.

Fish and bread they threw away, though they understood that it was to eat, but when I showed them 2 pigs I had brought ashore they seized them by the ears like dogs and were for carrying them off immediately and would have killed them had I not stopped them. After they were gone I took the 2 pigs, which were a sow and a boar, about a mile into the woods and let them go beside a brook of fresh water. I would have left cattle, goats and sheep, but it was clear the natives would have killed them as soon as we had left. The pigs may survive long enough to breed, they being animals that soon revert to the wild and are naturally fond of the thickest parts of the woods.

We had no better fortune with the weather on Wednesday, the morning being dead calm, so we cut grass and wood again, the grass in one patch being plentiful and good. More natives came to the wooding party, including women with children, the women quite naked except for a kangaroo skin tied over shoulder and waist, but for no other purpose than to carry the children, which had fine features and were quite pretty. The women did seem possessed of some modesty, for they rejected the offers of some of the *Discovery*s men.

But this may have been through fear of displeasing their own Men, for an elder among them observing this ordered all the women and children away, the which order they obeyed with some reluctance.

The needs of our men, which are very natural after so long on board of the ships, is always a possible cause of trouble. In the islands of the Pacific this is not the case, the native men having not the same sense of possession of their women as seems to exist among races of colder climates. Much care has to be exercised in this matter by myself and the officers, for if the women are too forward in responding to the advances of our People, then there is jealousy which can transform a scene of peace so suddenly and so completely that our People have to be protected from the consequences of their own natural inclinations. This is something I am most reluctant to be involved in, since it can have fatal results and so affect the manner in which any ship that comes after me is received.

Calm and light airs from Eastward kept us anchored in the Bay until Thursday 30th when a light breeze at West enabled us to get to sea. Having done so, the wind veered to the Southward and increased to Storm. Of this we were warned by a fall of the Barometer, but then for a brief time it brought with it an intolerable heat when the mercury in the Thermometer rose in an instant from 70° to almost 90°.

The only captains to have visited this land before were Tasman, who discovered it in November 1642, and Capt Furneaux, who was there in the *Adventure* after he had separated from me in October 1773*. I have given the Latitude and Longitude of this Bay and also the Capes and Islands in my Journal. I have also said that New Holland, of which this land is the most southerly part, if it is not a continent must

* Cook did not know of Marion de Fresne's visit in March 1772.

be one of the largest, possibly the largest island in the World. We are now on the open sea passage to New Zealand where I shall hope to discover the exact cause of what befell Capt Furneauxs men. Some time during the night of the 6th and 7th the *Discovery* lost a Marine overboard, this being the second such man Capt Clerke has had the misfortune to lose since leaving England. He hailed me the following morning to inform me of the loss, the 2 ships then being in close company, both making very much the same speed through the water and this explaining why we had lost sight of his lights during the night, the which caused me some concern on being informed of it. There is nothing more disturbing when sailing in close company than to lose touch with the consort for no apparant reason.

17

NEW ZEALAND

Monday, February 17th

This last week and more I have been much occupied ashore and with my Journal in which I have set down all that I have discovered from the Natives I encountered in Ship Cove. We are anchored in our old station in Queen Charlottes Sound, which we reached at 10 in the Morning of Wednesday 12th February, having first sighted the coast of the Southern Island of New Zealand on the Monday and rounding Cape Farewell some 45 miles to the north the following morning. No sooner had we anchored than several canoes came alongside, but few of the men in them ventured on board, they being afraid that we had come to revenge the deaths of

Furneauxs men. This I learned from one of them whom I had befriended when I was last here, he having learned from a conversation he had had with Omai that I was well aware cf the bloody affair. I did my best to reassure them and in this I appear to have been successful in that they laid aside the distrust they first had of me. This does not altogether surprise me for the attitude of these people to death is one of acceptance as something ordinary even though the means be violent, so accustomed are they to warring among themselves and to the eating of human flesh.

By the 13th we had set up our Observatory and begun making observations to determine the rate of the Timekeeper, as well as having the empty casks ashore for water and 2 men appointed to cut spruce and boil it to make an essence from which we shall have spruce beer to refresh us during the voyage ahead. A great many families came from different parts to reside with us, putting up temporary dwellings with remarkable facility, the which provided Mr Webber with abundance of subjects for his brush. Some of these natives went out fishing every day so that by exchanges we never wanted for fish, living with great enjoyment off something that was not unlike a small salmon. Every day Sellery and scurvy grass was boild up with the Portable Soup, Pease & Wheat for both ships companies, with spruce beer to drink. We had visitors in addition to those who resided with us, and these traded for curiosities, fish and women, so that all the time I had Marines posted to ensure that we did not at any time suffer the same fate as poor Capt Furneauxs men.

Because I cannot prevent it I allow my People to have intercourse with women when it is proffered and the Native men do not object. But I do not encourage it for though it is a sound practice for men settling amongst a people to take one of their women, we are not settlers but travellers and having connection with women with no regard for them, but only a selfish need to satisfy an appetite, there is always the danger of anger and betrayal.

Last Saturday I made an excursion by boat to look for grass and visited the Hippah or fortified village on the SW point of Motuara. This was where Mr Bayly had his observatory when the *Adventure* arrived first here in 1773. In their leisure hours they had planted gardens with seed brought from England, but no vestige now remained, they all being choked with weeds. Yet we found Cabbage, Onions, Leeks, Parsley, Radishes, Mustard and cress and a few Potatoes, these last being from the Cape and having been greatly advantaged by the change of soil. Husbandry, however, is quite foreign to these people, so that no attempt had been made to extend the gardens or to increase the produce we had been at such labour to bring them by planting of either roots or seeds.

18

THE TRUTH ABOUT BLOODY COVE

Sunday, March 2nd

We are at sea again, having weighed and stood out of the Sound 10 a.m. Tuesday last 25th February 1777, keeping company with the *Discovery* and sailing E through the Strait to take our departure of the land at Cape Palliser 2 days later, which is the SE point of the Northern island of New Zealand. We had been anchored in the Sound 12 days, which is I would think the smallest number in which we could have expected to re-stock with fresh victuals by trade with the Natives, cut all the grass we required for our animals and otherwise prepare the Ships for the voyage through the Pacific. We took observations for 11 of the days and by a mean of these the Timekeeper was too slow, losing at the mean rate of 2″,913 per day. The Astronomical Clock was also losing on Siderial time 40″,239 per day and we had a difference of 6′45″ by the Moon on the Longitude that Mr Wales had here last voyage, his being that much more to the West. Other opportunities will now have to be taken to make further observations.

Omai has added to our numbers on board by 2, he being from our first arrival in New Zealand determined to have servants with him to improve his circumstance and impress his grandness upon his return home. The eldest of these is a youth of 17 or 18 named Tiarooa and I thought little of it when he came on board, thinking that when we sailed he would return to his people. But this was not the case, he being the son of a Chief who was killed and eaten as is the savage custom of this Country. His mother is still alive and treated with the greatest respect, and she did come aboard just before we sailed to say goodbye to her Son and receive a last gift from Omai.

With this youth another came to be his servant, but having second thoughts he departed before we sailed, though he had slept on board all the time we were anchored. But the next morning his post was taken by Coaa, a boy of some 10 years old. He was delivered on board by his Father with as much indifference as he would part with a dog. This child was in tears before we left and was only prevented from abandoning Tiarooa by one of the Elders of the Tribe. Now they are both crying their hearts out, making of their tears a sort of lament in praise of their Country and their People, which is as much due to sea sickness as for their longing for home, and

I think it very wrong of Omai to have told them that they will be returned later in the voyage, since I do not know what lies ahead or how I shall return, whether by way of New Zealand or by a more direct route, or by that North West Passage, the which I am instructed to discover. And if not the North West Passage, then perhaps the North East Passage over the top of Russia.

Since we sailed I have been much taken up with making my official report in the Journal of the true facts relating to the massacre of Capt Furneauxs men in what he called Bloody Cove. I have certain observations to make on this that are personal and not suitable to state in my Commanders Journal. But so that these be properly understood I must first relate the facts as I have discovered them from Kahoura, a Chief that sometimes visited us, and also an old friend of mine whom we called Pedro, a man who had been almost continuously with us the last time I had been in the Sound.

Kahoura had actually headed the party who cut off Capt Furneauxs boat. He had himself killed the officer who commanded it. I talked to him and to others through Omai, which is something strange, he coming from an island so many thousands of miles away, the which supports my belief that all these Peoples of the Pacific are of the same race, moving from one island to another in their big seagoing canoes in the same fashion that we do in our ships. He was not much loved, but greatly feared as a bad man, and many there were who importuned me to kill him, which is something that is quite natural to them, they believing in the Old Testament law of an eye for an eye, and if I had I do believe they would have eat him there in front of me.

The cove where the *Adventures* cutter was overwhelmed is on the E side of the Sound. We called it Grass Cove because of the abundance of that commodity. Here Pedro met us with another, both armed with Pat'too and spear, but nevertheless showing manifest signs of fear. Whether this was out of courtesy or caution, they expecting us to revenge our comrades deaths, I do not know, but their fear was quickly allayed by some gifts I made them. They told us in some detail the circumstances in which the massacre had occurred. Capt Furneauxs men, of whom there were 12, had paused at their work and were sitting around enjoying their victuals, several of the natives close about them, when some of them snatched some bread and some fish, for which the sailors did beat them, and this being resented a quarrel ensued. In this disturbance 2 natives were shot, and in the instant the natives sprang upon all of them, either seizing them or knocking them on the head with war clubs. This before the 2 muskets could be reloaded or another, if there was another, could be fired.

Pedro then indicated by pointing at the angle of the Sun in the sky the hour at which it had happened, which was in the late afternoon. He also showed us the exact spot where the crew had sat to eat and where the boat had laid about 200 yards away with Capt Furneauxs black servant in it. Later we were told that it was this man who was the cause of the trouble in that when a native stole something out of the boat he dealt him a heavy blow with a stick, whereupon the fellow cried out to his people that he was killed. There are other versions; that Mr Rowe, the officer, fired upon the thief and killed him and that this brought People out of the woods who got between our men and the boat, Mr Rowe firing and killing another of them before all were overwhelmed. Yet another, which we had from Kahoura himself, that on offering a stone hatchet for trade to one of the boats crew the man kept it without making payment, whereupon the natives snatched bread from them as recompense. This I believe to be a lie to make our People appear the cause. But the rest seems true enough, that Kahoura was hidden by the side of the boat and that when Mr Rowe shot the chief, he seized his opportunity before the musket could be reloaded to attack Mr Rowe, who drew his Hanger and wounded him in the arm before he was overwhelmed.

That the whole Melancholy affair was unpremeditated is clear and the Moral of it is in dealing with all Natives it is to be constantly remembered that our laws do not apply. Where there is no conception of property as we understand it, that is to say that there are many simple peoples to whom the possession and ownership of things has no meaning, then the greatest circumspection must be exercised. The use of force is seldom wise when ashore and faced with overwhelming numbers, though they be indifferently armed. The only sensible way to deal with any instance such as this I have recounted is through the Arees or Chiefs of the Tribe, by seizing upon their persons or persuading them of the trouble there will be for their people if items that belong to the Ship are made off with.

19

THE NATURE OF TRIBAL WARS

There are I will admit great differences in the nature of Peoples and Tribes of different parts of the World. The tribes of these islands of New Zealand are the most warlike I have encountered, constantly fighting among themselves, each tribe so determined on the destruction of another that even in the short time I was in Queen Charlottes Sound I was

constantly being importuned to go to war in aid of this
village or that or to avenge the death of our People which
they considered to be our natural duty and inclination,
and I do believe that even when Omai explained to them why
I did not do so, they did not comprehend. Omai himself
did not understand, arguing with me that if a man kills
another in England he is hanged, so why did I not hang
Kahoura? He could not believe that I could forgive and
wished my visit to be one of friendship, he being not over
gifted with imagination and the total concept of our voyage
quite beyond him.

This is a very different attitude to the peaceful nature of
those people I found upon the Society and Friendly Islands,
which were the names I gave to those that were the furthest
north I ventured in the Pacific on my last voyage, the which
I shall certainly call upon again to re-victual upon our way
north and to leave with them some of our animals.

I had intended leaving a bull and 2 heifers together with
sheep, goats & hogs, in New Zealand, for the number of
livestock we carry is a constant source of concern to me and
the cause of much labour to the crews of both ships in cutting
grass whenever we are anchored. I knew also that water
would be an even greater problem when we got into hot
weather latitudes. But I could find no Chief powerful enough
over all the tribes to protect them, and of those I left there
on my last voyage in West Bay and Cannibal Cove there was
no sign, though I was told there was poultry gone wild in
the Woods behind Ship Cove and I did hear that a Chief
named Teratou had a great many Cocks & Hens and one of
the Sows Capt Furneaux left ashore. Teratou was not there
at any time while we were anchored and, as evidence of the
unending struggle for power among the tribes and their
terrible warlike nature, I learned that another Chief, Tringa-
boohea, was killed about 5 months before we arrived together

with some 70 of his people. No man's property is secure in this country, but having before left upward of a dozen pigs in this Country I do not think they can have failed to breed and some survive. Two minor Chiefs soliciting me for pigs & goats, I let them go to take their chance hoping for the best.

On the matter of war between Tribes I would only say that it is a form of feuding, they being continually watching out for revenge, sometimes over many years, no Son ever forgetting an injury done to his Father. They creep up on the others when they are unguarded at night, sparing neither the Women nor the Children, and having slaughtered them they do then feast upon their bodies on the spot, gorging themselves sick, or sometimes taking away as many bodies as they can carry to their own home where they eat them, committing all sorts of brutalities upon the corpses. They take no prisoners nor give no quarter, but if they are discovered upon their raids they creep away and vanish into the woods. Thus all must be constantly upon their guard, having both Body and Soul to preserve, for should any man be eaten he goes straight to Hell, descending down into everlasting fire. But if he is killed and his body saved from being eat, then his Soul goes to Heaven, ascending upwards into the abode of the Gods. So their beliefs of Heaven and Hell are not much different from ours, and they also accept that a man has a Soul. Moreover, they bury their dead as we do and regard with abhorrence the thought of eating their own people after saving their bodies from the Enemy, but if they have more of the Enemy dead than they can eat, then they do not bury them, but throw them to the fish in the sea.

They have Priests who alone may speak with the Gods, but they do not gather together to worship in publick, the meeting house being for practical discussions. They cut their hair off and do sometimes fast with it, but for what reason I do not know except that it is connected with Eatua and is a ritual matter. But though they are for ever warring among themselves, a stranger journeying through their land is safe so long as his stay be no longer than that required to conduct the business upon which he is come. This ensures that they may trade their greatest possession, which is the green stone they call Poenammo which is found somewhere in the region of the southern island. There are many fabulous tales about this stone which is much prized, one being that it is a fish which when caught and brought ashore turns to stone. All agree it is fished out of a large lake or collection of Waters, the which I take to mean that it is a stone from the mountains that is brought down by torrents. All the southern island is known by the Stones name and called by the natives Poenammo*.

Of more interest to me were the stories I had of them about the medicines and unguants they extract from roots and plants, in particular a relief from the Pox. They say this disease was brought in a ship that came to their land only a few years before we first came there in the *Endeavour*. They called it Tupias Ship, but they may have confused the time or it is even possible they may in some polite way have been referring to our own ship, except that it would have meant a considerable elaboration of the tale in that they claimed the Captain during his stay kept one of their women and had by her a son who was still living and now about Coaas age. It was by this ship they said they were infected with the Venereal Disease, but that it was now less common and the effect of it not near so bad as at first. Their method of cure was to wrap the sufferer in green plants that had first been

* This greenstone, even now a tourist attraction and not unlike jade in appearance, is found in the Arahura river on the west coast of South Island.

laid over hot stones, thus forming a poultice that gave off steam like a bath*. I would much like to have gone further into this matter of medicine, having been somewhat troubled of late by pains in my leg which I fear is some form of rheumatism, due probably to the long months spent in the cold Southern Seas on my late voyage and brought on again by the damp of our quarters and the fogs we experienced after leaving the Cape. It is something I must keep to myself, for if I showed any of my People that I was in pain they would have less confidence in me than they do, the Commander always of necessity having to appear superior to those afflictions that do normally plague human beings. It is at these moments that I think with some longing of my home in Mile End Old Town and of my wife who would as always be of such great comfort to me.

* A hot poultice is one of the basic Maori medicines. The practice of medicine among the Maoris was sufficiently advanced for them to carry out trepanning operations. Discussing this with Hepe Te Hao Hao, one of their paramount chiefs, he told me he had been cured of terrible back pains by such a poultice after European doctors had abandoned his case as incurable.

PART FOUR

Pacific Islands

20

SLOW PROGRESS

Tuesday, April 1st, 1777

All Fools Day and hoping the land we had sight of yday at Noon will afford us better prospect of an anchorage than at Mangaia, the island we reached on March 30th and which we found hostile both as to the coast and at first the people, for our beasts are in great want of food. But we have little wind and making up toward this next island is slow work. The wind has been very fitful and exasperating all this past month.

For a fortnight after leaving New Zealand we had the wind mostly between SW & N, some times Strong Gale with hard Squals, at other times moderate so that we made good progress in the direction we wished to go, carrying all sail on a course of NE by E. We are thus in Lat. 39°29'S and Long. 196°04'E, our progress slow and all on board feeling the heat. The wind such as it was then veered between NE & SE so that we began to make too much to the Northward, our course for Otaheite* requiring as much Easting as Northing. By March 16th the ships log records the wind veered to N so that I was able to tack and stand to the E, but very light and some times Calm. It then freshened at ESE so that we could again stand NE, but only for a short time as it often veered to E or even ENE so that we frequently made no better than N and even Westward of that course.

* Tahiti, the island group to which Cook was ordered to return Omai.

We did not cross the Tropic* until March 27th and then only in Long. 201°23'E which was 9°W of our destination. I had thought all this time I would have been experiencing Westerly winds otherwise I would have made more to the Eastward after leaving New Zealand. The whole month has proved one of great frustration, always expecting winds we never got, and our progress so slow that I begin to have considerable anxiety about making the coast of North America in time to explore Northward before the ice begins to form.

I do not believe as some do that ice only forms from fresh water. It is true that the ice formed at sea, as we discovered in the Southern Ocean last voyage, yields fresh water when it is melted. But the sea does freeze off the E coast of North America. This I know, so that even though it be all water to the Northward of that continent, it will still turn to ice in winter and so stop our progress beyond Capt Behrings strait.

All March we saw nothing of any birds that would induce us to think we had passd close by any land, only a Tropic bird, also a large tree, but so covered in barnacles that it could have drifted on the currents from almost anywhere. The sellery and scurvy-grass &ca we took on board in Queen Charlottes Sound, together with the diet of Portable Soup and Sour Krout that we carry and also the hygiene I practise, all on board washing themselves every day in sea water and both ships constantly aired and the periodic smoking of all parts below deck, has preserved all in reasonable good health, only the animals being a matter for concern.

On the 29th the *Discovery*, which was to the NE of us, made the signal for land in sight. This was at 10 in the

* The Tropic of Capricorn which is Latitude 23½°S.

Morning. It was an island of no great size and by Sun set it
bore NNE about 2 or 3 leagues so that we were forced to
stand off and on until Day break when we could see a great
surf breaking every where with great fury upon the reef
and no way in to any anchorage. A great many inhabitants
made their appearance out of the woods brandishing long
pikes or clubs. After searching the N side of the island and
finding no harbour of any sort, we turned back and met the
same 2 men in a canoe that had come out to us before. This
time they approached near enough to receive presents lowered
to them on a line. I then had a boat lowered and went to
them and they came alongside, stepping into my boat without any fear. I ordered Omai to question them about a
landing place, but the two they indicated would have been
a great risk to our boat, so we reconnoitred ourselves to
within a cables length of the breakers when we had 40 to
20 fathoms depth over sharp Coral.

While we were thus engaged great numbers of the inhabitants all armed thronged upon the reef, but the man I
had in my boat, who was some sort of Chief, ordered them
back so as not to hinder our landing. This man came back
with me to the Ship, but very uneasy all the time he was on
board, which may be the reason that he expressed no surprise
at anything we showed him, except that on leaving, as he
came out of the Cabbin, he fell over a goat, staring at it
astonished and asking Omai if it were a bird.

This island was called Mangaia and I departed from it
with great reluctance, it being well wooded with Bread
fruit, Cocoanut, Plantains & Tarra root so that it would have
provided us with all fresh provisions of which we were in
need. And the people not unfriendly, though their actions
and language come nearer to the New Zealanders than the
Otaheiteans, but their colour between the two and their

ears pierced with large holes like the people of Easter island, one with a knife stuck in the hole which Mr Webber did make a drawing of.

Now with another island in sight I am hoping that we shall not again be disappointed of a landing for we are in great want of refreshment.

21

THE COOK ISLANDS

Sunday, April 13th

We have now touched upon 3 islands and got very little for our trouble. Light airs all the time and so little water that I have had the still kept at work. Some improvement has lately been made to this Machine, but I do not regard it as such, it yielding no more than 13 to 16 gallons of water though it was at work one day from 6 in the Morning til 4 in the After noon. My concern for the cattle is great, having transported them all this way and no opportunity to put them ashore, which was my intention. And the winds being so tedious I am now disappointed in my original intention, having in 2 weeks made barely 4° of latitude to the North-ward.

The first of the 3 islands was Atiu, which Omai called Wenua-no-Eatua, meaning a land of Gods, for he said many of the men on it were possessed of the spirit of Eatua, the which causes a kind of frantickness common in Otaheite and neighbouring islands. The 2nd was Wennuaete, which signifies little island; and the 3rd was Manuae, which I had visited on my last voyage and called Herveys island after my friend of the Board of Admiralty Capt Augustus John Hervey who is now the Earl of Bristol. There was no anchorage at any of these, but at Atiu Mr Gore with Omai, Dr Anderson and Mr Burney from the *Discovery* were ashore in a canoe, in some peril of their lives they thought, being surrounded by a multitude of people, then pent up for the whole day and in the evening much alarmed when a fire was made, Omai in particular being afeared they were to be roasted and eat. But it was only to roast a hog and all were returned safe to the ships well fed, but nothing in the way of trade.

It was on this island that Omai met with some Otaheiteans who, sailing in their canoe to the island of Ulieta, had missed it through poor navigation or other adverse circumstances, and after being at sea a great number of days, their canoe was oversent. Only 5 out of the 20 men and women survived, they being much weakened by lack of water and victuals but still clinging to the side of the oversent canoe until it was drifted toward Atiu, the people of which sent out canoes to bring them in. This I believe is the way in which these people, who all speak and behave in much the same manner, have progressed through the Pacific, their colonisations being not so much by intent as by chance. Omai offered these castaways a passage back to Otaheite with us, but they declined, saying that they were better suited where they were.

Mr Gore also landed on the small island, this time in our own boat which I had ordered ashore if it were at all possible. Despite the great surf breaking upon the rocks he, with the Jolly boat as well, brought off Scurvy Grass and Palm leaves, about 90 Cocoanuts and branches of the Wharra tree*, which being of a soft spongy juicy nature we fed to the Cattle who did eat it very well though it was much like feeding them billit-wood. We made no landing on Herveys island,

* Pandanus.

for after I had sent Mr King to reconnoitre in one of our boats, he was met at the outer edge of the reef, which was a quarter of a mile from the shore, by some of the inhabitants armed with long pikes and clubs, and observing that their women were very busy bringing down more spears and darts, he returned. We were in great want of grass for the Cattle and also of water, neither of which could be procured from any of these islands without great labour and some danger.*

22

AN INEVITABLE DECISION

Reluctantly I made the decision to bear away from the Easterly wind and make for the Friendly Islands,† which were to the W, knowing from my previous Voyage that they would give me good anchorage and provide us with all that we were in such urgent need of. It was not a decision arrived at on the spur of the moment, the which I fear some of my officers will have a misapprehension of when they learn of our ultimate destination. But none of them have experience of the North American coast and so cannot understand how early and how suddenly the Winter does come upon that land. For some weeks now the realisation has been growing on me that we were too late in starting upon this Voyage and the Summer already too far advanced in the northern Hemisphere to enable us to prosecute those discoveries in high northern latitudes for which I am

* This small group of islands at which Cook had so little luck, are now named for him the Cook Islands.
† Now known as the Tonga Islands.

committed, we not yet being across the Equator, after which we have no less than 60 and more degrees of Latitude to make to the N.

The decision I have now made, which is to postpone the search for the North West Passage until next year when we shall have the advantage of all the time we require, is a great disappointment to me. I could have stood back to the S until I had the advantage of westerly winds, but it would have meant the loss of all the Cattle, which I still have hopes of landing to the advantage of the peoples of the islands, and even then I think we would be too late in arriving in the Strait, so it is likely no advantage gained and the animals all lost. Besides which, in our haste to make to the Northward, I fear we should consume too much of the Ships stores and provisions. I do blame myself, not for the decision, nor for any failure to make as much haste as possible on the Voyage, the winds having been more contrary than I had expected, but because I failed to appreciate when I was in England how urgent it was to get to sea betimes and make a start upon the Voyage.

It is better, I am convinced, to proceed upon this expedition with caution rather than to endanger all our lives with reckless haste. And there is some advantage to me personally in that I can now utilise the summer months for a proper study of these island People, the which I have not had the opportunity before. There is so much about them that fascinates me, they being navigators of no mean sort and their customs, nature and practices being all so interesting. This I shall set down in my Journal with as much detail, and I hope with the greater facility that comes with the practice of writing to which I was at one time quite a stranger, that it will be very acceptable to that larger Publick which requires always to be entertained with details of the life of the people, their religion, morals and most intimate practices. For the next few months therefore I will concentrate upon the Journal with the intention of setting down the fullest possible record of these People, the which has not been done by any person heretofor.

I shall not write any of it here that is not to my purpose, this being a very private account of my thoughts and deepest concerns, but if at the end of the Voyage this record should be considered worthy of publication, either during my life or perhaps more properly after my death, then whoever shall prepare it for the press can add as much to it as is thought necessary from the official account in my Journal. It was Dr Douglas who made this suggestion to me that I should set down my most intimate thoughts, so that there was more in it of the person I am, and something also that Mr Boswell said to me. I have had in mind therefore that I am writing to that kind and considerate friend and employer of mine Mr Walker of Whitby. And if there is any choice of who should correct all my various mistakes in spelling and punctuation, and give to it that polish of phraseology the which he has achieved in his own writings, I would hope perhaps I might prevail upon Mr Banks, with whom I am glad to say I was during my stay in England on the most friendly and even affectionate terms despite all that had gone before when preparing for my second voyage, he being disappointed of the command of it and much angered thereby.

23

PLANS
FOR THE NORTH

Wednesday, November 19th, 1777

We have now been in the Friendly and Society islands all
of 6 months and with Winter coming on I think it time for
me to leave Omai and proceed upon the main purpose of
my voyage. Accordingly I have this day delivered my
Instructions to Capt Clerke how he should proceed in the
Discovery in the event that we become separated after leaving
these islands. We will shortly be exploring coasts that few
if any save the Greek navigator Juan de Fuca have touched
on before. And since I cannot know whether I, or any of us
if the truth be admitted, may survive I am copying my
instructions to Capt Clerke into this record, as I did my
original Instructions, so that if the *Discovery* be lost and I not
survive, it will be known how I made provision for our
meeting up upon the coast of New Albion.*

By Capt James Cook Commander
of His Majesty's Sloop Resolution

Whereas the Passage from the Society Isles to the Northern
Coast of America is of considerable length both in distance
and time, and as a part of it must be performed in the very

---

* The west coast of America north of California, which was
then occupied by the Spanish and which the Admiralty had
expressly ordered Cook to avoid. It was named Nova Albion by
Drake who discovered it in 1579.

depth of Winter when gales of Wind and bad Weather must be expected and may possibly occasion a Separation, which you are to take all imaginable care to prevent. But if notwithstanding all our endeavours to keep company, you should be separated from me, you are first to look for me where you last saw me, not seeing me in five days, you are to proceed, as directed by their Lordships Instructions (a Copy of which you have already received) for the Coast of *New Albion* endeavouring to fall in with it in the Latitude of 45°; in which latitude, and at a convenient distance from the land, you are to cruze for me ten days.

Not seeing me in that time, you are to put into the first Convenient Port in or to the North of that latitude, to recrute your wood and water and to procure refreshments. During your stay in Port you are constantly to keep a good look out for me, it will therefore be necessary to make choice of a Station situated as near to the sea-coast as you can, the better to enable you to see me when I appear in the offing. If I do not join you before the 1st of next April, you are to put to Sea and proceed northward to the latitude of 56° in which latitude, and at a convenient distance from the coast, never exceeding fifteen leagues, you are to Cruze for me till the 10th of May.

Not seeing me in that time, you are to proceed Northward and endeavour to find a passage into the Atlantick Ocean through Hudson or Baffins Bays, as directed by the above mentioned Instructions. But if you should fail in finding a Passage through either of the said Bays or by any other way, and the Season of the year may render it unsafe for you to remain in high latitudes; you are to repair to the harbour of St Peter and Paul* in Kamtschatka, in order to refresh your people and pass the Winter.

But, nevertheless, if you find you cannot procure the

* Petropavlovsk, or as Cook spelt it, Petropaulowska.

Necessary refreshments at the said Port, you are at liberty to go where you shall judge more proper, taking care before you depart to leave with the Governor to be delivered to me on my arrival, an account of your intended destination. And in the Spring of the ensueing year 1779 to repair back to the above mentioned port, endeavouring to be there by the 10th May or sooner.

If on your arrival you receive no orders from, or account of me so as to justify your pursuing any other Measures than what are pointed out in the before mentioned Instructions, your future proceedings are to be Governed by them. You are also to comply with such parts of said Instructions as have not been executed and are not contrary to these orders. In case of your inability by sickness or otherwise to carry these and their Lordships Instructions into execution, you are to be carefull to leave them with the next officer in command who is hereby required to execute them in the best manner he can.

To

   Captn Charles Clerke

   Commander of His

   Majesty's Sloop

   Discovery

Given under my hand on board the Resolution at Ulietea* the 18th day of Novr 1777

         J. Cook

Now I must recount some of my chiefest concerns during the half year we have sojourned in the islands above mentioned.

* Cook's spelling of Raiatea.

24

WOMEN AND THIEVES

First as regards the People under my command. Such a long period of relative inactivity must always put a strain upon the Discipline of the Ships. I do know that they look upon me as a man of undoubted severity and this I have never discouraged. Indeed, it is something I have at all times fostered, both in my manner and bearing, my officers all being much younger men and only myself by practice and experience able to enforce Discipline by a glance. I am seldom able to relax, nor have been these many years, so that when I see myself in the mirror I am forced to the realisation that by habit my features have become set into an expression that is something severe. Capt Clerke manages to temper this with his humour, but I lack this advantage, and if I be not much liked by some it does ensure that I am always obeyed and so absolute master in my own house, though living in close company with others long years at a stretch. Nevertheless the strain of it is at times almost beyond bearing and when I see the flaunting, libidinous behaviour of some of the women of these islands, they so handsome and free with their favours, I confess there are moments when I would be happy to exchange the isolation of command for the carefree abandon of a Midshipman's life.

It is this knowledge of my own weakness that causes me to turn a blind eye to the presence of females on the ship. I do not openly condone it, but pretend not to know. There are two or three living aboard at this present time, one of them seemingly with such great attachment to Mr Edgar that I do believe he is half in love with her, so that if he were

not the *Discoverys* master but only a seaman he would desert
the ship. Others will certainly attempt it now that everyone
knows our destination and the conditions that will face us
during this Winter and next Summer in the high latitudes
of the Northern Hemisphere. But I have not lost a man yet
by desertion, nor do I intend I shall on these islands or at
any place we touch upon on the American coast.

It was but last week we had the latest desertion. Moored at
Haamanino Hbr in the Otaheitean island of Ulietea I had the
Observatory set up and all the instruments taken ashore so
that Mr Bayly and I could observe the Suns Azimuths both
on board and ashore to discover the Variation. This we did
on the 7th and 8th November and on the night of the latter
observed an occultation of S. Capricorni by the Moons dark
limb, Mr Bayly using the Acromatic Tellescope, Mr King
the Board of Longitudes Reflector and I my own 18 inch
Reflector. And then on the night of the 12th and 13th the
Marine posted as sentinel over the Observatory deserted
taking his Musket with him. Having myself discovered which
way he went, I sent a party after him, but they returned in
the evening without seeing or hearing anything of him.

In such circumstances it requires that I go ashore, talk with
the Chief and apply to him to send a party of his own people
after the deserter. This I did, and because there were many
natives around the Ships engaged in their usual thievery,
all were taken with *matau*, which is to say a dread of my
presence, and vanished, including the Chief. I had intelligence that the man was at a village called Hamoah on the
other side of the island and I went there with 2 armed boats,
apprehending the Chief on the way. This was all that was
necessary, our party beaching the boats about a mile and a
half away and marching briskly over land, whereupon they
took me straight to the deserter, whose name was John
Harrison. He was in one of the houses, sitting between 2

women who burst out crying at my arrival, and his Musket was lying on the ground.

I have ordered him to be disciplined with a dozen lashes on each of 2 days, this being the maximum allowed per day for a single Crime. Two dozen lashes is not a great punishment, my anger and annoyance being tempered by the circumstances that he had stayed at his post till within a few minutes of his time of release. I do believe that had I gone ashore alone, without any armed party with me, it would have been sufficient for me to apprehend him, for the natives of these islands do hold me in great dread and awe, but whether from my manner and habit of command or for fear of the reprisals I may inflict upon them I can never be sure. My purpose, however, in recounting this escapade is to indicate how troublesome are the natural desires of my men, requiring of me time and energy that would be better employed in observations and all the other objects of the voyage.

Discipline and punishment is something all men on a voyage of this nature learn to accept, recognising the need for it if we are to return safe to our own Country. John Harrisons desertion was a momentary lapse, largely on account of the lure of those women and the attractions of this place. It is something I can understand and forgive. Thievery I can never forgive because, while desertion affects only the deserter unless he be allowed to get away unpunished, the theft of Ships stores affects the safety of us all and endangers the voyage, Nails and other larger items not being obtainable anywhere and therefore irreplaceable. The temptation thus to satisfy their lust is understood by Capt Clerke and myself, this being the price the Women demand for their favours, and having suffered such deprivation from previous voyages we take great care to guard against it. But whilst thievery of this sort I can understand,

I was myself appalled when we were beating north from New Zealand to have the midshipmen and some others of the crew complain that their victuals were being stolen.

This is something I had not suffered on previous voyages and it is the most damnable thing. It is like a sore, the thieves feeding upon the body of the crew and if unchecked the whole infected with suspicion and anger. Since we could not discover who the thieves were, I had recourse to something that is the last resort of those in command; I had the whole Ships company assembled and told them that unless the thieves were informed upon I would on the next occasion that meat was stolen reduce the Allowance to $\frac{2}{3}$rds the following day. This having no affect, I did reduce the Allowance, whereupon the men refused to eat it, complaining of the injustice of being punished for a crime they did not commit, all of them being entirely honest. Considering their behaviour near mutinous I informed them the $\frac{2}{3}$rds allowance would continue indefinitely and that thereafter the meat would be issued after it was cooked and not raw. That ended the matter, but it was not to my liking since it confirmed the poor opinion I had of some of the men shipped for this voyage, the thieving being secret and without the knowledge of the rest.

This was in April when we were very short and only the week before I had had my own sheep killed, and also those belonging to the gunroom gentlemen, so that the men should have some variety and the officers not appear to be better supplied in this respect. But while the men behaved unreasonably and very near to a mutinous proceeding on this occasion, they behaved most sensibly when on our arrival at Otaheite I called all hands together and having acquainted them with the purpose of the voyage and the improbability of renewing any of our Provisions, I did suggest to them that it would be better for the present to discontinue the daily issue of Spirits and preserve our Grog for those colder climates which were our destination the following year.

It is not my normal practice to submit my intentions and desires to my crew, this being a Navy ship and not a private venture, as was the case with many of those earlier Discoverers who deferred to a Council for the wishes of a majority. However, the issue of rum and other spirits is a Custom that gives every man something to look forward to each day, a relief from the burden and routine of his close confinement, causing him to relax and so enjoy the company of his fellows instead of becoming resentful and argumentative. On this occasion I had the considerable satisfaction that no sooner had I put it to them that they saved their Grog for when the harshness of the climate made the issue of it more necessary, they without the least hesitation or a moments consideration did agree and consent to it immediately.

I have written of thieving on board, but much more difficult to deal with and most troublesome is the thievery practised by the natives of all the islands we have visited. It seems common throughout the Pacific, and though I go ashore everywhere and arrange the trade, putting an officer in charge of it as I did Mr Banks on that first voyage in the *Endeavour*, and setting the terms of the trade, the thievery continues very troublesome so that everything must be secured and the People watched at all times.

When we were at Nomuka in the Friendly Islands we caught one of the *eiki* or chiefs making off with the bolt of the Spun yarn winch, for what purpose I do not know since it was little use to him but of importance to us as it was upon this machine we made our ropes. I ordered him a dozen lashes, then took him ashore securely and most uncomfortably tied to the place where we traded and did not release him until I had a hog given me for his liberty. Thereafter no Chief engaged in thievery, but always they employed their servants or slaves for this dirty work on whom a flogging made no more impression than upon the Main-mast, and when we caught them as often as not their masters advised that we kill them. This I would not do and since my customary punishment had little effect I often did not bother to punish them at all. Capt Clerke conceived of a better idea and had their heads shaved, or the half of it, so that they were marked out and as a result derided.

However, there is no stopping their thieving, and not only in the Friendly Islands, but in the Society Islands also and at Otaheite itself, so that the constant necessity to keep watch on everything about the Ships when there were natives on board or in their canoes which so often swarm around us proved most wearying, and always I did my utmost to maintain a degree of impartiality between the islanders and my own People, so that I found myself as previously in the Pacific having to stand in judgment whenever there was conflict between the two. This was sometimes to the disadvantage of my seamen, particularly when it involved the women who infested the Ships, as was the case when a Tongan chief whom I greatly respected came on board of the *Resolution* and wanted to take away a Girl he found with one of my sailors between decks. The man had paid the price for her favours for the night, which was a hatchet paid to her father who had delivered her on board, and so refused to give her up. The Chief insisting and attempting to drag her away, the man struck him, whereupon the Chief made complaint to me. I had no alternative but to order the man a flogging, this Chief being second in importance on Nomuka and my orders being very strict that no man shall strike a native of any degree for whatever reason. This is a most necessary regulation for the avoidance of provocation and the attendant danger of stirring up enmity and so endangering all our lives, for we are most times greatly inferior in numbers. Our superiority in weapons is something to be relied upon only as the last resort, since knowledge of our actions and behaviour travels fast by canoe through these islands and we greatly depend upon the goodwill of the natives for our Provisions, thereby saving the Ships stores for our greater need in the Northern Hemisphere.

Thievery and women are a constant annoyance to me and the greatest disadvantage of these most salubrious attractive islands, the former having to be guarded against at all times for the danger it may inflict upon our enterprise and the latter accepted by me because I must. If the men were not contented in this manner there would have been Mischief, by which I mean desertions, even Mutiny, for having lost this year I had no alternative but to stay in these islands where we had all we needed in the way of Provisions.

The constant intercourse with the women, both ashore and on board of the Ships, some of them even voyaging with us from one island to another, is a danger both to themselves and my own People. I have always ordered that no man shall be permitted to stay a night on shore who has the Venereal, but there is always the difficulty that neither Mr Anderson, the surgeon, nor, I declare, any member of his Faculty, can truly declare a man free of the disease, since it is so normal a complaint of sailors and they, though possessed of it, often appearing able-bodied in every respect. In cases we know of my orders do ensure that it is not communicated to the islanders. But the native Chiefs are not so concerned and I have no means of enquiring into the health of all the Women that come aboard.

The discovery I made upon visiting the Friendly Islands this time that the people there were infected by the disease indicates how impossible it is to prevent the spreading of it. Some of our own People were so infected of the Venereal after we had left and I did myself see when I was ashore natives who had ulcers on their bodies, others with the nose or parts of it missing. They do not regard it of great account, which surprises me, so that I am inclined to think that they were inflicted of the disease prior to my visiting the islands on my last voyage since such a short interval of time would seem to be insufficient to produce so dreadful a disfigurement.* When the swellings are sufficiently big to cause a tumour they make deep gashes across it with a sharks tooth or other sharp instrument. Some have swellings of the legs and arms for which they apply a piece of sinew tied very tight to prevent it spreading. This is not the Venereal but something else, very near as shocking to look upon.†

Whatever the cause of these people being infected with Venereal I intend to hold very strict to the precautions I have always taken wherever we may anchor so that so far as is possible I cannot be accused of having brought our own disease to the islands. I can do no more, and if the Spaniards or the Russians, or anybody else, have been there before me my conscience in this matter will be free of any guilt.

* Possibly yaws or even infection from cuts caused by the coral when swimming.
† Obviously elephantiasis.

25

A CURE
FOR RHEUMATICS

I was myself suffering at this time from the rheumatics, the pain beginning at the hip and extending right down to my heel. Though I kept more than usual to the Cabbin it was not possible for me to hide my affliction from the Ships company, the pain being very great and myself unable to move without limping. Then in September, when we had been among the Otaheitean islands a little over a month, I was forced by my affliction to decline an invitation made to me to attend a *Morai*, which is a thanksgiving to the gods of Otaheite. The invitation came by Messenger from Towha, who had returned with his fleet of war canoes after concluding a Peace with Mahein, a rival Chief. I would much like to have attended this ceremony, but instead sent Mr King and Omai, myself returning to the Ship. With me in my boat came the Mother of Otoo, another chief, and his 3 sisters with 8 other Women. I thought at first they had come on board to take passage with me to Matavai Bay, but so soon as we were on board they said they were come to sleep there and to cure me of my pains.

Many who read this will profess astonishment that I accepted their offer, but my voyages have revealed to me that there are many peoples who we would regard as primitive and uncivilised that have developed most remarkable cures from the plants and roots that grow in their lands. I had beds made up for the women in the Cabbin and submitted myself to their ministrations, though I would have thought twice about doing so had I known what they intended. I was desired to lie down in their midst, the which I did, whereupon as many as could get at me began to squeeze my flesh, using both their hands and working upon my whole body, though more especially upon the area of pain in my leg. They made by their onslaught a perfect Mummy of my body, squeezing me till my bones cracked. This first attempt lasted a full quarter of an hour and when it was done I was much relieved to be rid of them. Nevertheless, the pain was less and before I retired to bed they were at me again so that I had a fairly comfortable night. The cure was repeated in the morning before they went ashore and again in the evening when they returned to the Ship, and after that I had no more pain.

This operation they call *Romy* and though sometimes performed by men, it is more usually the women. They use it upon themselves whenever one of them is overtired or languid and this has a very good effect, particularly upon the legs, as I discovered myself, always thereafter benefiting from this treatment.

These people, whether of the group of islands I called Friendly, or that I named after the Society, or here in Otaheite, are not at all like their distant relatives in New Zealand in that they do not appear to practice cannibalism, but the gods they worship are similar and they are warlike, on certain occasions as I witnessed making human sacrifice at their *Morai* or secret place, but using a corps and not killing a man for the purpose . . .

26

TAHITIAN NAVAL TACTICS

Monday, November 24th

Having been moored to the shore at this place, we took the opportunity the ground being good to heel the Ship and scrub both sides of her bottom, so that I could not any longer write unless I went ashore to do it. At the same time I have had them fasten some Tin plates under the bends, which are the thick planks that do girdle the sides of her just above the waterline. These plates were provided by the ingenious Mr Pelham, Secretary to the Commissioners of Victualling, as a substitute for Copper. The Copper sheath is laid over the extra planking that is studded with large-headed nails to give something of an iron protection, but since those parts of the Copper that are worn or damaged cannot be replaced, Mr Pelham thought to try Tin as a protection against the worm. Whether it will serve the same end as Copper we shall only discover by attempting it.

The work is done now and as well as it is possible to do with the men clinging like flies to the slanted sides of the ships. The worm does not seem to affect the native canoes, of which there are very many, this being their mode of travel, of transporting people and goods, and of fishing along the outer edges of the reefs. Either the material of which they are constructed is not to the taste of this pest that seems to inhabit all the warm waters of the Globe or they discard their canoes or repair them as soon as ever the worm infects the wood. The canoes are double-ended and vary from the

smaller *va'as* or *proeses* to the great war canoes which are 60
or 70 feet long with a rounded bottom made of large logs
hollowed out to a thickness of about 3 inches, the sides
being built up of planking of similar thickness.

Some 2 months ago I was offered one of the former by
Otoo just before we sailed from the island of Otaheite to go
to Moorea. It was about 16 feet long and having all those
pieces of Carved wood upon it that they do fix upon their
war vessels I thought at first it was a model of one such,
but it was a *va'a* and being much decorated I would have
taken it with me except that it was too large to be conveniently stowed. Their war canoes are of great interest to me and
a little before, when all of those at Matavia were paraded
for a general review, the Royal family having arrived with
presents for our Ships so bountiful that we had more on
board than we could dispense with, I took the opportunity
to get some insight into the manner of fighting them.

I having made my request, 2 of the fleet were ordered
off, Mr King and myself with Otoo in one and Omai in the
other. When we were out in the Bay, we faced about, both
canoes advancing and retreating by turns as quick as the
paddlers could move them. The warriors upon the Stages or
fighting platforms brandishing their weapons and display-
ing all sorts of Anticks, the purpose of which seemed to be
to arouse their fighting passions. Otoo stood at the side of
the Stage giving the order when to advance and when to
retreat. After moving thus backwards and forwards upward
of a dozen times, the 2 vessels closed bows-on so that the
Stages were held fast together and after a mock fight it was
declared that all our men were killed and Omai and his group
boarding us, Otoo and all the paddlers leaped into the sea at
the very same moment to save their lives. Omai informs me
that this is not always the tactic employed, but that sometimes

the 2 canoes are lashed together head to head, in which case they fight until all the warriors in one or the other of the vessels is killed. It seems that if this is the method adopted, they never give any quarter unless it be to hold an enemy for a crueller death next day.

For their safety these islands and each community relies upon its Navy of war canoes, never fighting upon land but only upon the water so accustomed are they from birth to the sea and the manoeuvring of their vessels. The night before a battle is given over to feasting, the place of the engagement having been agreed by both sides in advance, and since the victor spares neither women nor children, those who have lost can only save themselves by fleeing into the mountains. This is the manner in which lands and sometimes whole islands change hands, and after the slaughter the winners all assemble at the *Morai* to give thanks to their gods and to Sacrifice the Corps of those that are slain and also the prisoners if any be taken. Omai declared that he was once taken prisoner by the men of Bolabola* and would have been put to death next day if he, and the others with him, had not contrived to make their escape.

Our mock battle over, Omai donned the Suit of Armour he had brought with him from England and mounting a Stage on one of the canoes had himself paddled all along the shore. But though he was standing in full view of all I think he was much disappointed in the attention paid to his demonstration.

I will write more about Omai, but cannot now as I have just heard from Capt Clerke that 2 of the men in the *Discovery* are missing and must go ashore to enquire of the natives. I would not mind so much except that one of them is Mr Mouat, Midshipman and son of Capt Mouat who was a

* Cook's spelling of the island now known as Borabora.

commander at Quebec in 1759. Though but 16 years of age the boy should have learned better from his father than to desert ship, if that is what he has done, led astray by some Woman.

27

ALARMS, EXCURSIONS AND A PLOT

Wednesday, November 26th

Having been up much of the Night observing an Immersion of Jupiters 3rd Satellite with Mr King and Mr Bayly, they using the 3½ foot Acromatic and I my own 2 foot Gregorian Reflector, I am in no mood to accept any longer this delay in getting the 2 deserters back. It seems that Mr Mouat had publickly expressed his desire to stay in the islands and that the evening preceding Capt Clerke informing me they were missing, they had gone away from the *Discovery* in a canoe. Of this we were informed by the Natives as also that they were at the North end of the island. Capt Clerke immediately went after them with 2 armed boats and a party of Marines, returning that same evening without even any certain intelligence as to their whereabouts. By this conduct he assumed that the Natives were harbouring them, they sending him off here and there in what can only be called a wild goose chase.

Next morning, which was yesterday, we were informed they were at Otaha, whereupon I decided I must go after the

2 deserters myself, knowing full well that there were others in the Ships desirous of setting up their home ashore in the islands and if these 2 Miscreants were not quickly apprehended there would be more desertions. Also the Natives, holding me as they do in very great awe, seldom venture to deceive me with false information. Accordingly I set out with 2 armed boats, having the Chief with me so that he could direct me, the which he did so that we did not stop until we reached the middle of the East side of Otaha. There we set a man on shore to go before us with orders to have the deserters seized and held until we arrived with the boats.

All of this proved a great waste of time, for when we arrived there we were told our men had left the day before to go to Bolabola. I thought it less than prudent to follow them in the boats and so returned to the Ships, resolving to adopt my usual practice of making the Chief responsible for seeing that they are brought back. So this morning, when he did come on board, together with his Son, Daughter and Son in law, I arranged for the 3 last to be detained, Capt Clerke luring them on board his ship with the offer of knives, where he confined them in his Cabbin. When their Father heard of this, he protested to me, thinking it was done without my knowledge, and when I undeceived him on the matter, telling him it was done on my orders, he made great haste to leave my Ship. I did not have him seized, but told him he was quite at liberty to leave but that the others would be held until the Deserters were returned to me, and if they were not returned, and the enticement of others to leave the Ships did not cease, I would not hesitate to carry his family with me when I sailed, which I was already preparing to do.

The whole matter was a most tiresome business, for though the Chief sent at once to Bolabola requesting Opoony, the

Chief there, to apprehend the deserters and send them back, a party of natives seized upon Capt Clerke and Lt Gore who were walking ashore a little way from the Ships. This was between 5 and 6 this evening. I was myself ashore and noticed all the natives who were in and about the harbour and the Ships suddenly moving away as though in a panic. The reason for this was not clear to me until they called out to me from the *Discovery* and told me what had happened. This was my own plan in reverse, the tables turned upon me. With no time to deliberate what to do, I instantly ordered the Ships companies to arm and within three or four minutes had despatched a strong company under the command of Mr King to rescue them, also 2 armed boats I sent after the fleeing canoes, and another party under Mr Williamson to cut off their retreat to the shore.

The seizing of our People or the sudden killing of them by these hot-blooded and sometimes warlike people is something I do often dread and fear may happen as it did to Capt Furneauxs people. But on this occasion it was a mistake, or not all of it as I discovered later when I had sent to recall both men and boats. Capt Clerke and Lt Gore were safe, but only because a fat jolly girl that was on board of the *Discovery*, having been brought by one of the officers from Huaheine, overheard some of her country men plotting to seize them and ran at once to inform our People. Also when the alarm was given and I had despatched armed boats after the dispersing canoes some shots were fired to stop them, and on hearing the report of the Muskets the party of natives armed with clubs that was coming up to Capt Clerke and Mr Gore turned on their heels and dispersed.

When I enquired into the circumstances of this plot, I discovered that the true intent had been against my own person. It was my custom every evening to go for a bathe in the fresh water that came down from the mountains, and in this exercise I was often alone and unarmed. They had expected me to go this evening and would have seized me then, and Capt Clerke if he had accompanied me which he sometimes did. But after I had confined the members of the Chiefs family on board of the *Discovery* I resolved not to go and cautioned Capt Clerke and the officers to keep close to the Ship for fear of some reprisal. The Chief came to me several times, asking if I would not go to the Water, but when he realised that I would not he went off with the rest of his people and nothing I could say would stop him, which I now realise was because he was a party to the design, if not the instigator of it.

This affair gives greater credence to the story that was whispered to me when we were at Lifuka in the Friendly Islands. I did not believe it at the time, partly because I did not wish to, thinking perhaps the people more friendly than they were, and partly because I would have had to forego a *bomy* or night dance with torches which I greatly wished to attend for the purpose of my Journal. It concerned a native named Fenough who had first presented himself to me as the Chief, but who I later discovered was no more than the 2nd and regarded by many of his people as a bad man. Whether there was a plot or not I do not know, it being something I heard later and the dance proceeding as I have described in my Journal without anything untoward happening. The supposed plan was to cut down myself, my officers and the guard of Marines at this dance, this being proposed by the Chiefs, but Fenough objecting on the grounds that it was better done by day when detachments could be led astray in search of me until the Ships were so weakened of their complements that they could be taken by assault. Fenough had that Morning desired to see the Marines go through their exercises, and he being gratified by me in this and the Marines firing off several volleys, he may have been discouraged. But if I listened to all the tales that were current in the Ships I would have become so feared of the Natives that I would have had to forgo all opportunities of studying them and their customs, which was my purpose in these islands.

That the people in these parts are warlike and sometimes treacherous I do not doubt. Oft times they behave like children and yet they are men and have their politics and the Naval power to force their will upon others of their country men. I enjoin caution upon all my People, but mixing so close with them as we must it is difficult to maintain such a guard that would keep us safe against all surprises and I rely greatly upon the awe in which all natives of the islands that I visit do seem to hold me, treating me always as a great Chief or even some sort of god. But whether that is because of my nature and behaviour or because of the power I have in my Ships and the discipline of my men I must leave to others to judge. At all times I endeavour to mingle friendliness with severity, maintaining absolute impartiality as between the natives and my own people, but it is their thievery that I do find most tiresome, so that I am not so much troubled for my own safety as for the property that is on board of my Ships and without which if they had taken something important we could not very easily continue our voyage.

28

TWO DESERTERS

Sunday, November 30th

We got away from Ulietea on the 27th, having carried everything that was on shore on board of the Ships, with the intention of following the Chief Oreo to Bolabola in search of our deserters. But the wind did not serve and the same wind that kept us in harbour brought Oreo back from that island with both men, who instantly had irons put upon both their legs and will stay confined while we continue in the islands. Shaw, who is aged 23 and a Gunners Mate, Capt Clerke has ordered disrated and he has been given 2 dozen lashes laid on very hard. Mouat will do duty before the Mast for the rest of the voyage. And that is the end of it, the vexation being more than the men are worth, particularly the boy, whom both Capt Clerke and I looked upon something as a son and who will now, by this one stupid action, make his distinguished father miserable.

The only good to be got of the affair is that the capture of them and the severity of the punishment meted out has had the effect upon everyone that I desired, the seamen petitioning their Capt to excuse Shaw further punishment and all hands promising to behave exceeding well for the future. One other good has come of it also, that Mr Webber has had the opportunity whilst she was held hostage to paint the Chiefs daughter, Poedua, who is very beautiful. And I am glad to say that some friends of the girl who gave the alarm, when the attempt to seize my two officers was made, carried her off in the middle of the night and took her to a place of safety until they could arrange for a canoe to take her back to Huaheine, the men charged with the execution of the design having threatened to kill her if she had gone openly ashore.

29

OMAI ABANDONED TO HIS FOOLISHNESS

Before all this happened I was intending to write something about Omai who we have now finally bid farewell to and left behind, not in his own island of Otaheite where he made too many enemies and had so much of his possessions taken from him, but at Huaheine. About this he seemed never able to make up his mind, for no sooner was it settled and the Chiefs met that could give him some protection than he desired to go on with me to Ulietea. This I would not permit, since it required that the Bolabola men that were in possession of the island be driven out and I told him bluntly that if he went there it must be as a friend and not an enemy. Whereupon I was told by one of the Elders that the whole island of Huaheine and everything in it was mine and I might give any part of it I wished to Omai. That settled, Omai began to behave in a more sensible manner, tending seriously to his affairs and seemingly to repent of the prodigality of his behaviour at Otaheite, which was the cause of so much envy and so much loss of his property. Nor did he show off by dressing up in every thing he possessed.

Accordingly I had the Carpenters set to work to build him

a small house, and since the relatives he had upon the island, which was a Sister and Brother in law, were not of a standing to protect either him or his property, so that he was liable to lose everything as soon as we had gone, I advised him to take a good part of his possessions to the principal Chiefs. Had he done this he would have ensured their protection, but I heard later he did not heed my advice and so is dependant for his protection against the envy of others less well endowed than himself upon my threatening to return to the island later, when those that were his enemies would feel the weight of my resentment. And so we left him and the natives in no doubt that I would return, which is something I cannot be sure of.

He did not seem at all disposed to take a wife, though the house we built him was 24 feet by 18 and 10 feet high, fashioned out of boards with as few nails as possible so that there might be no inducement for them to pull it down. He still had of his possessions a Musket, Bayonet and Cartouche box, a fowling piece, 2 pair of Pistols and 2 or 3 Swords and Cutlasses. I gave him about twenty pound of powder, some Musket cartridges and pistol balls, though I think he would have been better without them. He was such a silly fellow in many ways so that I often had cause to regret that Capt Furneaux, if he must bring a native back to England and with so many good youths to choose from, had not carried off a more sensible. Yet he had his good points, being very likeable and sometimes useful since he could inform us what the people were saying and was always grateful of the favours he received in England.

I have written this of him in my Journal: He had a tolerable share of understanding, but wanted application and perseverance to exert it, so that his knowledge of things was very general and in many instances imperfect. He was not a man of much observation, there were many little arts as well as amusements amongst the people of the Friendly islands which he might have conveyed to his own, where they probably would have been adopted, as being so much in their own way, but I never found that he used the least endeavours to make himself master of any one. This kind of indifferency is the true Character of his Nation, Europeans have visited them at times for these ten years past, yet we find neither new arts nor improvements in the old, nor have they copied after us in any one thing. We are therefore not to expect that Omai will be able to interduce many of our arts and customs amongst them or much improve those they have got, I think however he will endeavour to bring to perfection the fruits &ca we planted which will be no small acquisition. But the greatest benefit these islands will receive from Omais travels will be in the Animals that have been left upon them, which probably they never would have got had he not come to England; when these multiplies of which I think there is little doubt, they will equal, if not exceed any place in the known World for provisions.*

The two boys that Omai took on board in New Zealand I would have taken with me, this being their wish, but that I did not entertain much hope of another ship being sent out from England to bring them home. So we left them also, one of them being so attached to us that he had to be carried ashore by force. Before we left we exhibited some of Omais fireworks, much to the delight and wonder of the great crowd of natives that were gathered to see them, and also some expressions of fear.

It was two days later, some time between 12 and 4 in the Morning, that a man who had made himself a mortal enemy of Omai, and who for Omais safety I had in confinement,

---

* This was not the case, Bligh recording on his voyage in the *Bounty* that all but the pigs and dogs were dead.

contrived to make his escape, taking with him the shackle of the bilboo-bolt that was about his leg. Upon enquiry I discovered that not only the Sentry, but the whole watch on the quarterdeck had laid themselves down to sleep, so that he was able to take the Key of his irons from a drawer. It was clear no proper lookout was being kept at night and for an example to the others I had the Mate of that watch, Mr Harvey, disrated and sent on board of the *Discovery* as a midshipman and Mr Martin, one of Capt Clerkes midshipmen, brought on board the *Resolution* and rated Mate. Mr Mackay, the midshipman of that watch, I sent before the Mast, he and Mr Harvey being both in bed during the watch, and since the Sentry and the Quartermaster appeared guilty of aiding the escape they were flogged a dozen lashes on each of several days. In this manner some of the Marines were also punished, this being something that cannot be overlooked if we are to have a safe voyage.

The night before we left Huaheine, I and all the officers, except Capt Clerke whose health was very poorly*, dined ashore with Omai, when we were served with the very best the island afforded. Before we departed I had this Inscription carved upon one end of his house: *Georgius tertius Rex 2 Novembris 1777 Naves: Resolution Jac. Cook Pr, Discovery Car. Clerke Pr.*†

* He was already suffering from the tuberculosis he had contracted during his period in prison.

† Pr is short for *Praefectus*, *praefectus naves* being the Latin for Captain of a ship.

30

THE COMMANDER'S RESPONSIBILITIES

It is with relief that I am now able to turn such energies as are left to me towards the object of this Voyage. My enforced stay in these islands, though of benefit to my official Journal, has proved most fatiguing and a great burden upon my resources, the which has been increased by Capt Clerkes sickly state of health, though in all other respects I could not wish for a better nor a more pleasing officer to have with me in command of our consort. All these six months I have felt the weight of my responsibility to maintain discipline among my own People as well as to ensure their strict behaviour towards the natives, so that there be no reason nor excuse for them to fall out with us. During such a long period with oft times so little for our men to do the danger is boredom. This is something that seldom occurs on a Vessel of War, not even during a blockade, for they are at sea and the crew in watches and so pretty fully engaged.

On this voyage that I am sent upon the temptation to desert and otherwise behave in a manner that is contrary to the Navys practice and discipline is very great and it is upon the Commander that rests the whole weight of maintaining that sense of purpose and endeavour that alone can carry the voyage to a successful conclusion, and this as much by his own self-discipline and manner at all times as by the strictness of his regime. Yet he must at the same time consider the happiness of his People, so that they do not hate him to the extent of conspiring to mutinous proceedings, but only respect him and hold him in some awe. I do relax sometimes, when I am bathing or feasting with the natives, their manner being so exceeding cheerful and friendly that on occasions I attend wearing nothing but my breeches, unarmed and with my head bare so that my hair, which is now bleached almost as white with the sun as the coral sand, hangs down to my shoulders. Officers of a seventy-four or some such ship of the line would be very surprised to see me then, but I cannot always be on my guard, month after weary month.

And it is not only the maintaining of proper discipline and constantly looking to our safety ashore or at anchor that is tiresome. I am informed by the people of these islands that there are sometimes great storms that come tearing down upon them with very huge dangerous seas and I have seen some evidence of these where palm trees have been snapped off and whole villages destroyed and abandoned. This gives me some cause to believe what they say and, besides maintaining our observations, must always have an eye to the weather so that we may take action in advance to save our ships, the anchorages not always being very secure, though the best we can find in islands that are more often than not surrounded by coral reefs.

However, the health of my People is very good and except for the Venereal and those diseases of the Tropics that are to be found here we have suffered very little Sickness. They have the advantage of all manner of fruits and vegetables, also fish from the sea, including turtle which they have much sport in catching, so that I have at no time had difficulty in the provision of a proper diet. I hope I will find as good upon the American coast, but knowing the scarcity of such provisions on the East side of that continent, I do not think it very likely.

31

AN ISLAND
FOR CHRISTMAS

Tuesday, December 30th

We are now at a very barren low island with but a few shrubs
and plants growing out of a black soil that would seem to
be composed of the dung of birds and decayed vegetables
mixed with the coral sand. In places it is bare of anything
but coral stones and shells thrown up in long narrow ridges.
These are like fields ploughed parallel to the coast, but sometimes well back from it so that I think it incontestable that
the whole island is formed of Marine productions and
continues in a state of increase. There is no water to be had
here and those who have drunk of the Brackish pools have
suffered bad results of it. The island is some 16 miles long
and almost as many across, which is larger than I have seen
before of islands formed totally of Marine creatures. But at
our first sighting of it, which was on the 24th about half an
hour after day breake, it appeared only as a low bank with a
few Cocoa nut trees enclosing a lagoon.

This sort of island is very common in the Pacific, and a
great contrast to Bolabola which was a very high mountainous island. After leaving Bolabola I steered to the Northward
close-hauled, the wind being generally between N and NE,
and some time in the night between the 22nd and 23rd we
crossed the Equator in the Longitude of 203°15′E. Before
leaving the Society Islands I enquired of the inhabitants
whether there were any islands to the N or NW of them, but
they declared they knew of none. It is thus evident, though

they progress 2 or 3 thousand miles southward across the Pacific, that for some reason they do not sail their canoes in this direction, for on the 24th about ½ an hour after day breake this land was sighted. The wind being ESE we only had to make a few bords to get up to the lee of it when we anchored in about 14 fathoms fine sand some ½ a mile from the breakers.

The next day being Christmas Day I named this island Christmas Island as I had called the place where we spent Christmas last year in the Kerguelen Islands Christmas Harbour. I sent a boat from each ship to seek out a landing place and 2 others to fish. These last caught 2 hundredweight of fish between day breake and 8 o'clock. After breakfast I sent them out again and myself went in another boat to search for a way through the reef, but found none. About noon Mr Bligh returned with the first 2 boats I had sent and reported a Channel into the lagoon about a league and a half to the N of us, but only fit for boats, the whole lagoon being very shallow.

As the previous year, we could not hold our festivities on the proper day but kept Christmas Day on the 26th, the People being served with fresh pork from the Hogs we had from Bolabola, also fish and a double Allowance of Spirits. Having reports of turtle in the lagoon, and of the green sort which are very good eating, I ordered Capt Clerke to send a boat out hunting for them in the SE part of the lagoon while I, with Mr King, went each in a boat to the NE part. We saw but one, which we caught, then waded through the water, which was not very deep, to the small sand island that is at the entrance to the lagoon. Afterwards I left Mr King to observe the Suns Meridian and went inland, walking to the sea coast where I saw 5 turtle swimming close inshore, only one of which we caught, but it was the exercise I enjoyed after the hot tedious passage to the Equator.

The men are in great spirits, there being no inhabitants here and no need for any strict regulations. As many as can be spared from the Ships are sent out hunting for turtle, which gives them good sport, so that they forget what lies ahead on the voyage and give themselves up to the full enjoyment of this most barren island. I and Mr Bayly have been occupied in other directions, for this morning there was an Eclipse of the Sun to be observed and we began our preparations 2 days ago. This was the chief cause of my anchoring at this island for such a length of time.

The results we obtained this morning were not very satisfactory, the Sun being clouded at times and toward noon the heat of it reflected from the sand very great. Also there was a protuberance in the Moon, which escaped my notice, so that though Mr Bayly and I were both observing with the large Acromatic Tellescopes which are of the same magnifying power, there was a difference in the time between us of 26 seconds. Mr King was observing with the reflector and Capt Clerke would have assisted but that he was in such poor health that he was incapable of the effort. I am greatly concerned about his condition, there being nobody with his experience among my officers and if anything should happen to me the great weight of responsibility for the conduct of the expedition falls upon him; if his health do not improve I am doubtful that he can survive the rigours of the fog and ice we shall encounter to the N of North America.

32

FUN AND STUPIDITIES ASHORE

Sunday, January 18th, 1778

We weighed from Christmas Island at day breake on the 2nd and this Morning raised an island bearing NE by E with more land bearing N seen shortly afterward. But we have light airs and calms now so that it will be some time yet before we make up to it and discover what sort of a land this is.

During the week we were anchored off the lagoon at Christmas Island we took on board of the 2 ships about 300 turtles, which is a most providential addition to our provisions. They weigh about a hundred pound apiece with the shell and all the people engaged on the hunting of them had the greatest sport in getting them. With those that are on the shore sleeping it is but a simple matter to turn them on their backs and leave them thus helpless for the boats to collect. But when they are in the water, where they are to be found waiting in deep pools for the return of the tide, they are in their own element and very powerful so that often they escape into deep water beyond the reef.

Most of our men though not myself included are the best of swimmers and there is much merriment over the chase. There is some danger also, for there are numerous sharks, they being so voracious that they bite at the oars and even the rudders. The men who are fishing go armed with long pikes to hold these creatures off, and on board of the ships, when they are caught by those that are fishing with lines, they sometimes lash two of them together by the tails so that they cannot dive, which is called spritsail yarding them and causes great merriment.

It is very fortunate that we have not lost any men to these sharks, the biggest damage any has suffered being from the coral, the cuts being most difficult to heal. We did nearly lose 2 men, but only from the helplessness of sailors on shore who never seem able to look for what is obvious to any sensible man but become totally confused. The men were missing the last two days of December, the one for 24 hours, the other for 40 hours. The former saved himself by killing and drinking the blood of a turtle, which he also gave to his companion, but seeing that he was too weak to wander any further, he left him and finally joined one of the *Resolution*s boats. A search party found the other after walking some dozen miles or more across the island. He was in such great distress from the heat and lack of water, and also the burns that the sun had inflicted on his skin, that though revived with some bread and weak Grog he could scarce travel back to the boat.

Of this incident I have written in my Journal that it was a matter of surprise to every one how these men contrived to lose themselves, the land over which they had to travel from the sea coast to the lagoon where the boats lay was not much more than three miles across, and it was a plain with here and there a few shrubs upon it and from many parts of which the Ships masts were to be seen; but this was a thing they never once thought of looking for, nor did they know in what direction the ships were from them, nor which way to go to find either them or the party no more than if they had but just droped from the clouds. Considering what a strange set of beings the generality of seamen are when on shore, instead of being surprised at these men losing themselves we ought rather to have been surprised there were no more of them; indeed one of my people lost himself in the same place, but happening to have sagasity enough to know that the ships were to leeward, he got on board almost as soon as it was known he was missing.

The Latitude of Christmas Island is 1°59'N and the Longitude 202°30'E, which was established by as many observations of the Moon as there was time for. Besides Marine animals, there was on the island land crabs, small lizards and rats, and of birds Men of War and Tropic birds, Boobies, Terns, Curlews, Sand pipers and a small land bird like a hedge sparrow. Before leaving I had planted some Cocoa nuts and yams that we had on board and some Mellon seeds, and I left a bottle containing the inscription *Georgius tertius Rex 31 Decembris 1777* with the name of the ships and their captains as I had done at Huaheine. Most of the time we were anchored there we had fresh Easterly gale, but always a great swell from the Northward which broke in a very big surf on the reef, and this swell remained with us 2 days after we sailed, though the weather was fine with but a gentle breeze from the Easterly direction.

Not expecting to sight any land between Christmas Island and the American coast of New Albion, the day we sailed I set the Carpenters to work upon the caulking of the main deck and the following week once again had the Fearnought jackets and trousers served out. I also put the Ships companies to an allowance of 2 quarts of water a day per man, the wind being contrary and fearing a slow passage. Between Latitudes 10 and 11 we sighted several turtle and there have been birds with us every day, both which usually indicate land in the vicinity, but none that we saw until this Morning, when our position was 21°12'N, 200°41'E.

33

THE UNEXPECTED ISLANDS

Thursday, January 22nd

Our situation last Night and this Morning was none of the safest, the wind between SE and S with constant rain and ourselves so anchored that our stern is little more than 2 cables* from the breakers. We did not get to this anchorage on the second of the 3 islands† we had sighted til the 20th, having stood off and on all night. By then we knew the islands were inhabited, canoes having come out to us, and everyone surprised and gratified to find the natives had many words that were the same they spoke at Otaheite and the other islands we have visited so that our People could make themselves understood. And they had the same aptitude for thievery, or rather they thought they had a right to whatever they could lay their hands upon. Of this we had immediate example, the first man that came on board making away with the lead and line with which we had been sounding and taking it into his canoe. Another took the Butchers cleaver and leapd over the side with it.

This same desire to possess whatever they could get hold of was the cause of an accident ashore that was quite contrary to my orders and as a result not reported to me at the time by the officer in charge, which was Mr Williamson. Attempting a landing, he was prevented by the great number of inhabitants that came down to the boat. They pressed so

* A cable is 100 fathoms – i.e. 200 yards.
† These were the western islands of the Hawaiian group.

thick upon him, laying hold of oars, muskets, anything to hand, that he felt obliged to fire and so killed one of them. Mr Williamson is not the best of my officers and when I questioned him closely on the matter, he admitted that the natives did not seem intending any harm to our people, but were chiefly excited by curiosity and it was probably this that caused the man he killed to lay hold of his pistol.

It was such an incident as I have always used my best endeavours to avoid. I was very angry when I knew about it. These islands had water and we had taken on none since leaving Bolabola, which was 2 months since, and not to be told of it at once made it a worse offence. Finding the people friendly on our first acquaintance I did not order the degree of protection to those ashore that I would have done had I known of this incident.

There was at that time something I felt more important weighing upon me, not knowing that a man had been killed. When we arrived at these unexpected islands there were on board of the ships some that were suffering from venereal complaints, they having contracted the disease from the Women they had connection with in the Society Islands. There may well be others that we do not know about, for there are always some who will do what they can to conceal it from their fellows, being ashamed. And there are always men that do not care that they communicate it to the natives. We had an instance of this at Tongatapu in the Friendly Islands. The Gunner of the *Discovery* was put ashore by Capt Clerke to conduct trade with the natives and even when he knew he had contracted the disease he continued to sleep with different women, thereby giving it to them, or so they supposed. He continued in this manner despite the expostulations of his companions until Captain Clerke heard of it and recalled him to the Ship.

Accordingly, on our arrival here I gave strict orders prohibiting all intercourse with native women. No women are allowed upon the ships and no man is to go ashore in whatever capacity if he has the disease, is in any way suspected of it, or is off the Surgeons list as recently cured of it. The more serious of the men understand the reason for my orders, but the most of them have thought only for the moment and the pleasure they are deprived of, being quite incapable of imagining how others that come after us will regard our behaviour if they find we have introduced this fowl disease to people that were previously free of it. I have enjoined all the officers to maintain the utmost vigilance to prevent any intercourse whatsoever, but I doubt if we can prevent it entirely for some of these girls are exceeding wanton and abandoned and I have been told of occasions when they have endeavoured to drag our men into their houses by force.

I had reports of water here in ponds or shallow wells and as soon as we were anchored I went ashore with three boats to examine the supply and test the disposition of the natives. There were several hundred of them gathered on the sandy beach before the village and the very instant I leapd from my boat they all fell flat on their faces before me and did not rise until I had made a sign for them to do so. They then came to us with an abundance of provisions for the which they seemed not to want anything in return except my good opinion of them. From their behaviour it would seem the power I command of men and ships makes me appear to them a great chief or king.

The watering proceeded without any obstruction, the natives even assisting in rolling the casks to and from the pond. I took a walk up a valley accompanied by Dr Anderson and Mr Webber and a considerable retinue of the inhabitants, and everywhere I went the people prostrated themselves, lying with their faces to the ground till I had passed. There was in this valley a pyramid about 20 feet high which was some sort of temple, being in a *Morai* much like those of Otaheite with the same carved boards, but part covered by a thin grey cloth; something similar to this had been thrust upon me as I came ashore from the boat. Mr Webber made a good drawing of this edifice and later we saw others at every village along the E coast of the island. And at all these villages there was also many plantations of Tarra and Plantain, Sugar cane and the Chinese paper Mulberrry tree or cloth plant, so that, the people being so friendly and good natured, and so much in awe of me, we are not likely to go in want of provisions, pigs being in great plenty also.

34
SERGEANT OVERBOARD

Sunday, February 1st

Tomorrow I intend to sail. We are not yet full up with water, there being not too much of it to be had here and all to be carried off to the ships in the boats, but as we progress North-ward into Winter there will be less consumed than is required in the vicinity of the Equator. We have a full 3 weeks of provisions and a good diet to maintain the health of our People. This continued exceeding good considering all the circumstances, except that we have had an outbreak of the Yellow Jaundice. However, those that suffered from it show every sign of recovering fast and we have only lost one man, which is Roberts, the Quartermaster.

This man died the Morning of January 27th, having been sick of a Dropsy and unable to do any duty since we left England. I wish now that I had sent him home from the Cape for his death was very long drawn out and a sad sight to watch. I am also concerned for the health of Dr Anderson. He is in the same Consumptive state as Capt Clerke, and though both are at times sufficiently recovered to take a little exercise with me ashore, they are at other times so incapable that they are scarce able to undertake their responsibilities. Both would be a great loss to me, and not only for what they contribute to the expedition, but also for their companionship, so that oft times when I am alone in my bed I think of this, and about the meaning of death. This voyage is not like the others, for it has afforded me in my loneliness on board a great deal of time for reflection on matters that are too private to mention even here.

One thing I should mention is that on the following day I persuaded myself once again to carry my son Nathanials name on the Ships books as an able seaman, having carried both him and his brother James on the pay and victualling roll on my two previous voyages. This earns them time and myself something extra, and though some people may regard it as fraudulent, it is nevertheless very general and the custom among most captains. I had forgot to do this previously, James being now at the Naval Academy at Portsmouth and no longer needing to earn his sea time in this manner.

A more amusing matter to reflect upon occurred the Night of the same day Thos Roberts died when I was woken with the report of a man having fallen overboard from the *Discovery*. This was the Sergeant of the Marines who, being a little drunk with liquor, laid himself down upon the gangway to sleep it off. Both ships were under way at the time coasting along the islands and he slipping off the side of the *Discovery* into the sea one of the watch with great presence of mind seized upon a Machine that had been sent aboard in England to try, it being designed for just this very purpose. It is a pole with a weight at one end, a bell at the other, and corks to support a man in the middle. It was intended that the man that is overboard should sit in the corks and the movement of the waves would ring the bell, so enabling his rescuers to come to him. I had already tried out this Machine with our best swimmers, but they could never sit in the corks and the bell had to be rung by shaking the pole, the which the Sergeant did so bringing the *Discovery*s boat to him.

35

OF GODS
AND THE POLYNESIANS

This morning I got off Mr Gore and his party that was marooned ashore. I had sent them to trade with the natives on Friday and a gale springing up they were kept there 2 days by a very heavy surf falling upon the beach. This was the thing I had most wished to avoid, there being some 20 men ashore 2 nights including the Marines to guard them and as a result intercourse with the women very likely. Even the natives durst not venture out to us in their canoes and I only rescued our people by ordering Mr Gore to march his men to the SE point where they could be embarked. I took this opportunity to give some Goats, Pigs and seeds to a man who seemed to be in some command. At the same time I took a little walk into the island and when I stopped to look around a woman called to the natives that were with me, whereupon the Chief began muttering something like a prayer, and the 2 men that were holding the pigs walked round and round me. Thereafter many natives came to me from all parts of the island and all at a word from those that were with me laid down and remained with their faces to the ground until I was out of sight.

This behaviour of the natives of these islands is very strange. It is also somewhat disturbing, for in their manner they have raised me to a station that is entirely beyond capability of fulfilment. Their gods I know to be strange gods and something beyond my understanding, but that my person should be regarded in this fashion is to place me in the awkward position of not knowing what I am in their eyes and what they would have me be.

In the circumstances, I was not a little relieved that the gale forced me to get under way. This happened about 7 o'clock this evening, the anchor starting so that the Ship came off the bank on which we were anchored and no alternative then but to get the cable in and hoist sail. Now, thinking back to the visit we have made to these five islands, I have to remark upon the similarity of their people to many others of the South sea islands. They have a darker hue than the Otaheiteans, which may be because they wear less clothing, but I have no doubt they are of the same nation. So how shall we account for this nation, finding them as I have from New Zealand in the South to these islands in the North, and from Easter Island to the Hebrides? They are thus stretched out over 70° of latitude north and south, and 83° of longitude east and west, and how much farther I do not know, but west beyond the Hebrides I have no doubt; a great square of some 1300 leagues each way.

It is a most extraordinary range of ocean for any people and considering the nature of their craft and the squals that infest the whole region, there can be little doubt that these are the greatest navigators of any race, not excluding my own, our ships being so much bigger.

PART FIVE

America
and the Arctic

36
DOUBTS AND HOPES

Sunday, February 15th, 1778

It is now two weeks since we left the islands, the longitude of them having been fixed by a total of 72 lunar observations. The *Discovery* had caught up with us by the 2nd and though the course I wished to make was NE we were forced to stand away to the Northward, the wind being Easterly and very fresh. On the 7th the wind veered south easterly so that we could steer our course, but on the 12th it veered round by S and W back to NE so that I had to tack and stand to the Northward again, our position then being 30°N, 206°15'E. We have had no sight of any further land and the temperature seeming very cold after so long in the Tropics, though the Thermometer still reads about 60°.

During this time there has been much preparation on board of both vessels for the harder conditions that lie ahead. The Carpenters have been working on the Boats, which were badly stove in the surf, the Armourers forging new keel bands, and I have the Sailmakers busy at the sails. A strange matter, and one that is very revealing of the manner sailors have of settling to a habit, the Ships company petitioned me to serve them Sour Krout, which I did, though for their health there was no need of it for they still had plenty of the provisions we got of the islands, particularly Yams. The cockroaches we got of the Friendly Islands will I hope disappear as soon as we are in colder waters, but the rats that came aboard of us more recently are a serious matter, Capt Clerke reporting that he is having to make good a large hole eaten by them in the Quarter Deck where he had Yams stored.

The handling of the Ship being taken care of by Mr Bligh, and I only concerned with the Noon observations according to my Instructions, this fortnight has been a time for reflection upon the matter on which I am sent on this Voyage and what may lie ahead for us all. The two maps* lie constantly before me, and I giving so much attention to them that I have every detail of the supposed coastlines of Capt Behrings straits clearly imprinted on my mind. More particularly I have lately been examining closely the map which Müller included in his *Voyages from Asia to America*, the which he has called *A General Map of the Discoveries of Admiral De Fonte and other Navigators, Spanish, English and Russian, in quest of a passage to the South Sea*. It is described as being by Mr De Lisle and dated September 1752. This shows a lake that Bernarda sailed across stretching 436 leagues in a NEasterly direction and also the Passage that De Fuca discovered ending in the so-called West Sea, the eastern extremity of which is blocked by a great range of mountains extending from California to about latitude 65°N. And there is Admiral De Fontes route across the North American continent, entering it by way of a river called the De Los Reys and proceeding by way of Lake De Fonte or Mishinipi through Ronquillo Strait & Lake to Hudsons Bay. And in the far north of the Map at about latitude 80° are printed the words *Mountains of Ice*.

The more often I look at this Map the stranger it becomes, there being some of it that I must accept, though the exactness of the positions of rivers, lakes and mountains must be in some doubt, and there is much else that I fear is no more than a part of the mapmakers art, being based as I know them often to be on reports that are not in any way confirmed and sections of coastline drawn in for no

* Those of Müller (1761) and Stählin (1774).

other reason but that they wish to publish a complete map and not a collection of unconnected sightings of land.

How is it possible to put any faith or credence in this pretended strait of a Spanish Admiral or the long voyage across an inland lake of his Captain Bernarda when by all accounts these Spaniards will claim anything to their own personal advantage and glory and for the satisfaction of those in Madrid who have sent them north from the Pacific colonies? The voyage that De Fonte made in 1640 I have no reason to doubt, but until I see his passage with my own eyes I will believe his Discoveries to be no more than vague and improbable stories.

What then am I to think of the voyage of the Greek Capt Juan De Fuca, which was even earlier, being made in 1592? His claim to have sailed across the American continent from one side to the other in 22 days is not something that I can believe to be in any degree accurate. But their Lordships do believe there may be something in it and being a Greek and his people so much of a seamanlike disposition, I cannot dismiss it entirely. But in all of this I fear there is too much of hope and too little of reality, all our own people having failed to find a way through from the Atlantic Ocean or, from the Pacific side, even to approach the latitude of De Fucas strait, the which is about 45°N.

Only the Russians, and in particular the Danish Capt Behring, have succeeded in proving anything substantial in this extreme north part of the Pacific. I have myself great hopes and expectations of finding a Passage. But all that has been said of it was, previous to my last voyage, said and claimed for the Terra Incognita of the Southern Hemisphere, and it may be that this will prove to be as great an illusion as the Southern Continent.

If that is the case, then I intend to prove it to be so, as I did with the other, so that no man will ever thereafter have to be sent north again on another such voyage.

And though I doubt the validity of anything printed upon the map of De Fontes Discoveries and do fear I may find that the Mountains of Ice may prove, to my great discomfort, to be the one exact and correct statement thereon, I shall still press forward into the Arctic Sea to the utmost of the Ships capabilities and my mens endurance. There is such a deal to be gained for my Country if I discover the Passage, and much that has been offered to myself if I am successful. Time will give me the answer, not these maps, not even Dampiers dream, who is a man for whom I have considerable respect.

Saturday, March 7th

This Morning at day breake we raised the Coast of New Albion, which is that part of the western coast of America that is north of California. The land is about 8 miles distant extending from NE½N to SEbyE, of moderate height and well wooded. Our position by the Noon observation is 44°33′N, 235°20′E. Prior to our sighting of it, we had seen few birds or Oceanic animals that would indicate land anywhere in the vicinity until yesterday Noon when we sighted two seals and a whale.

Now that we are upon the Coast of North America I feel a great uplifting of the spirits, having wasted half a year, or so it seems, and now at last finding myself set upon the threshold of that purpose for which I am come here. The wind is light and variable and we are standing NE to close the coast. From hereon we shall have it always off the starboard side until we are through those Straits and can turn our bows to the eastward towards home.

Tonight I am thinking of my Elizabeth and the family, praying that I have the good fortune to return to them direct across the North of the World. What a peal of bells would

ring out, what honour I would have, and some fortune too ...
but my hopes run faster than this sun-dried leaking ship can
sail and I know from experience there are more fowl winds
than fair and nothing is ever achieved but that you force
it through against much difficulties.

37

AMERICAN INDIANS
AND SPARS

Tuesday, March 31st

These last weeks have not been of the best, the weather
proving very fowl for which reason I have now named the
first point of land sighted Cape Fowl Weather. My greatest
difficulty was to discover a safe harbour, our search for it
being hindered by the weather and by that natural caution
that besets the Discoverer closing with an unknown land.
No sooner were we near to the coast than the wind came to
NW in Squals of hail and sleet, the weather thickening so
that I considered it best to stand out to sea again.

We made several attempts to explore the coast more
closely, but the wind was generally from the westerly
direction, hard gale at times with heavy squals, sometimes
with snow showers, the land here still being in the grip of
Winter. In this searching for some suitable harbour, which
is very urgent now for the water we need and also to repair
the ships after so long at sea, we made nothing to the
Northward and at one time were pushed so far to the Southward that a Cape we sighted was most probably that called

Cape Blanco, which was discovered by Martin de Aguilar in January 1603. During all this period we suffered extreme discomfort, the ship leaking at her upper works and all feeling the cold.

The wind continued between W and NW, storms and moderate calms succeeding one another by turns, until the 21st when it backed to SW becoming fairer and enabling me to stand to the NE, so recovering the ground lost and closing the land again. The sails were got out to dry and the Bread Room smoked with Sulphur to kill the cockroaches; there were also rats to hunt, which kept the men busy and entertained. Two days after the wind was back at W and NW, moderating at evening and veering S, which was always the prelude to storm with rain and sleet. These southerly blasts, which lasted but 4 or 6 hours before we had another gale from NW, was the only means we made up to the Northward at all.

It was not until the 29th*, when we were standing to NE, that we saw the land again. It was of very different appearance, full of high mountains, their tops white with snow, and as we closed it we sighted what appeared to be two inlets. I bore up for that which was in the NE corner of the bay we were in and after entering it and being twice becalmed, we finally anchored just before night fall so close to the shore as to reach it with a hawser. This coast is inhabited, the which we discovered even as we closed the inlet, having at one time as many as 32 canoes full of Indians about us and almost a dozen of these remained along side most part of the night.

* It was during this night that Cook sailed past the entrance to the Straits of Juan de Fuca. He had no means of knowing that the land he closed next day was not the mainland or that the 'Passage' de Fuca had discovered was in fact the seaway between Vancouver Island and the mainland.

They appear a mild inoffensive people and very ready to trade, mostly the skins of such animals as Bears, Wolfs, Foxes, Dear, Polecats, Rackoons, Martins and in particular the Sea Beaver*. In exchange they take knives, chisels, pieces of iron and tin, nails and buttons, in fact anything of metal pleases them greatly. But here is the same problem as we had in the islands, they being as light-fingered as any we had met with. We have had them with us all this day and on board they mingle with our people with great freedom and lack of restraint, but with their knives they can cut anything free that takes their fancy. Our boats are stripped of everything in a moment, and in a very wily manner, one fellow amusing the guard while at the other end his companions are pulling it to pieces. If discovered at once, and we usually did so for they appear very ready to impeach one another, the thief is very reluctant to return the article, often being induced to do so only by force.

If this is the measure of all the Indians we shall meet with on this coast, then we shall have much trouble securing our belongings and all that is on board the ships. At this present time it is near impossible to keep a guard upon everything, for I have had the Topmast struck and the Foremast unrigged in order to fix a new bibb in place of that which was decayed so that the deck is much littered with the rigging.

Sunday, April 19th

The condition of the masts, the which I last wrote about, is causing us all great concern. It is not only the sticks that are decayed, but also the lower standing rigging. After getting the Main rigging set up on the 11th, we next day attempted to get the Mizenmast out, but it was so rotten it fell while the mast was in the slings. I spent a whole day in the woods

* Probably otter.

with a party that was sent ashore to cut down a suitable tree and next morning we dragged it to the place where the Carpenters were working on the Foremast. But when the work on the new Mizenmast was almost half done, the stick was found to be sprung, which was doubtless caused in the felling of it, so that we had to cut down another tree and start again.

Today, being the first fair day we have had for a fortnight, we got up Topmasts and Yards and set up the rigging. This was the most of the heavy and difficult work done and if the weather holds I feel sufficiently at ease with the state of the ship to have a look at the Sound in the morning. I shall be glad of the opportunity to be free of the Ship for a day, my energies having been so much directed toward the problems of refitting, and the Indians having to be guarded against all the time. Every day we spend here is a day lost in making to the Northward, not knowing what we may expect there except that the Summer will be very short lived.

38

THE PEOPLE
OF NOOTKA SOUND

Sunday, April 26th

At last we are ready to sail, but this morning Tide and Wind was against us. After we had got the Sails bent on and the Observatory with all our Instruments back on board, it took two more days to put the Ship in a condition for sea and bring on board small spars and timbers we have cut for use during the voyage. When we could not sail I was so frustrated with the trick the weather played on me I took Capt Clerke ashore to visit an Indian village at the mouth of the Sound, where we were received in a most friendly and hospitable fashion.

Their houses are communal, and since they use them for cooking, sleeping and all natural functions the smell inside of them is most disagreeable, being a mixture of rotten fish, sweat and urine, and far worse than anything we experience on board of our ships even when, because of bad weather, we are unable to ventilate or even to smoake below decks. As in other villages, we were offered food, but what they eat and the manner in which it is served is not to my liking. Capt Clerke, who seemed very cheerful today, said if anything happened to us upon these shores it might be to our advantage to accustom ourselves to the diet, but he also refused to partake of what we were offered.

We came back to the ship about noon with a boat-load of grass and it was shortly after our return that one of the Indians that was on board jumped into his canoe with a piece of iron he had stolen. He refused to give it up even when I seized a Musket from the Marine that was on guard and threatened him. In the end I was so angry with the stupidity of the Man, he knowing full well what damage the weapon could inflict on him, that I fired it down into the canoe. In accordance with my orders it was loaded only with small shot so for his stupidity he and several others had their backsides peppered with it, and so we got the iron back and they left us in a less friendly manner than was usual.

It always seems to be the same, in every place we anchor, that sooner or later an example has to be made to protect our stores and teach the natives to respect our property. Shortly after this it fell calm so we let go our Moorings and proceeded down the Sound with the boats towing. About

4 this afternoon we were able to hoist in the boats and proceed under sail, a breeze coming in from the North and a
very thick haze with it. I expect a storm shortly for the
Mercury in the Barometer is unusually low.

Sunday, May 17th

The Sound we left on the 26th April I named King Georges
Sound, but the Indians called it Nootka Sound*. We were in
that Sound near on a whole month, the which I fear I may
regret, so much time having to be spent on work that should
have been done at Deptford before we left England. Now the
question in my mind is the same as it was last year, shall we
be able to get far enough to the North to open up the
Passage in time to have full advantage of the short Summer?
I think it necessary to have discovered the entrance to the
Passage, if such exist, by the beginning of August at the
very latest, the which is no more than two and a half months
away.

I fear we may soon have to rely upon the antiscorbutics
that are among our provisions, for we found but little
in the way of fresh vegetables in King Georges Sound. The
most benefit we had was from the forest spruce trees from
which we made beer, though a tolerable quantity of wild
garlick was brought us by the natives and this sweetens our
broth, and there was a firm root which is edible though
like to liquorice in taste. Of fruit I found Raspberry, Currents
and Gooseberry and will hope I can rely upon them and
possibly others to be ripening as we proceed North.

Some account of the Nootka Indians was written in my
Journal while we were in the Sound. They are a very different
people to all those we have previously encountered in the

* Nootka Sound is the name by which it is now known. It is
halfway up the west coast of Vancouver Island.

Pacific, most particularly for what they cover themselves with in this colder climate and in their gods. For their cloathes they depend greatly on the animals of the spruce forest, but they eat mainly fish and other Marine animals, these being coast Indians and most certainly different in their customs and behaviour from those described by Hearne and others of the Hudsons Bay Company that have explored the interior. Though friendly, they are very dirty both in their Persons and in the manner of preparing their Victuals, but of their gods I understand very little. They most commonly have in their houses very large images carved of wood and in human form of which they speak in a most mysterious manner, and when Mr Webber was intending to draw one of these there was a man who seemed very displeased, but later for iron or brass they would have let me walk away with any I wished for. If these are their gods they hold them very cheap for I now have 2 or 3 of the smaller.

The cause of my failing to learn much of the Government and Religion of these people is that I have none with me who can speak their language, and because it is of the greatest importance that I be able to communicate with them, I spent considerable time while at Nootka making a list of some of their words and the meanings thereof. This I did chiefly by signs, writing the answers down as best I could by the sound of the words they spoke. But while this may help to make our requirements known to other Indians we shall meet with, it will not suffice for me to make enquiry of them what ships have been on this coast and where I may find the entrance to the Passage leading through to the north and east.

This is my greatest difficulty and one that I am not likely to overcome.

39

REPAIRS AND
A POSSIBLE PASSAGE

For the last day of April we were in 53°22'N, which is the
latitude of the pretended Strait of Admiral de Fonte. But it
would not have been prudent to keep in to the coast, the
weather being very tempestuous, and so I cannot state with
absolute authority what I believe to be true, that the Geographers have been misguided about the very existence of
the los Reys river.

All the beginning of May we had fair weather, the calms
on occasion of such absolute serenity as I have seldom seen,
sky and sea appearing as one and everything reflected with
the clarity of a mirror, so that our progress has been slow.
Not until the 6th did we arrive at what I think to be Capt
Behrings anchorage, the latitude being 59°18'N which
corresponds pretty well with the Map of his Voyage. This
was after we had sighted a most remarkable conical mountain
which I named Mt Edgecombe, the snow pouring down from
its top like cream on a cake, all of which Mr Webber drew
most perfectly. At this point the coast began to trend more
and more in a westerly direction and at the same time our
fine weather gave way to fog and excessive hard squals from
SE.

All this time we had the coast close aboard and not only
for the purpose of mapping it. The ship had developed a
leak and I wanted to get into some anchorage where it could
be stopped. This I was finally able to do in a large bay or
inlet, heeling the ship at her mooring by Kedge anchor and

hawser. In laying out the Kedge one man had his legs fractured, being carried out of the boat by the buoy rope and dragged straight to the bottom. It is difficult to protect men from their own carelessness, but at least he had the good sense to disengage himself from the rope and come to the surface again. The Carpenters, on ripping off the Sheeting, found the leak to be in the seams, those both in and under the wale being very open and in some places devoid of Oakum.

On our anchoring in this inlet and my sending a boat to sound the head of it, there was an attempt by Indians armed with spears to take it. This being prevented, they moved to the *Discovery* and on climbing aboard and finding only the officer of the watch and a few others on deck, the ship appearing otherwise deserted for it was early morning and most were still asleep below, they drew their knives, making signs to the officer and others to keep off, and began looking for what they could take. They had already tossed the rudder of one of the boats down to their canoes when the men below, alarmed at what they could hear on deck, came up armed with cutlasses. That was sufficient to discourage the Indians and no Musket shot was fired.

It would seem from their boldness that these people have no knowledge or experience of firearms, otherwise they would not have dared attempt any such thing, which leads me to think that no other ship has been upon this coast.

We weighed at 4 o'clock this Morning with a light breeze from ENE and meeting with a good deal of fowl ground and the wind failing us, we had considerable difficulty extricating ourselves from the danger that threatened. The Channel of this inlet is about 6 leagues across and wide enough to be the entrance to some Passage, which I intend to explore, having now anchored again under the eastern shore.

40

DISAPPOINTMENT

Monday, May 18th

There is no passage here, or very doubtful. I sent Mr Gore with 2 armed boats up the northern arm and he reported it extending a long way to the NE. I then sent Mr Roberts one of the mates to sketch it and he was of the opinion he had sighted the end of it. Mr Bligh with 2 more boats returned from the arm that was easterly in direction to tell me that it connected with the inlet we were last in and one side of it was only formed by a group of islands.

Early this morning the wind came favourable for getting out to sea, so weighed at 3 a.m. resolved to waste no more time here. We are more than 500 leagues to the Westward of any part of Baffin or Hudsons bays and it is my opinion that any Passage must lie North of latitude 72°. The Indians have indicated that there is a way Northward to the sea that will take us 2 days, but this information being got by signs I cannot rely upon. Nonetheless, the Russians have indicated a line of islands to Westward and no doubt there is a passage through them to the N.

We are now seeking to get to sea by way of a Channell other than that we entered by, hoping it to be shorter, but there being many rocks above and below water we shall not have much rest tonight though it be fairly light.

Tuesday, June 2nd

This is the greatest disappointment yet. On May 26th we headed north into what I took to be another inlet, but some believed otherwise despite the high mountains ahead that were all capped with snow. Now I am proved right and no alternative but to turn back, the Master having returned after exploring all night with 2 boats and reporting the water ahead of us perfectly fresh. Much debris is also floating past on the ebb so that, though the distance between the two shores is still a league as far as Mr Bligh went, and still navigable, it is nevertheless a river. By this and its several branches it is clear a very extensive inland communication lies open, for already we have traced it as high as 61°30'N, to 210°E, which is over 70 leagues from its entrance. I shall call this the Turnagain River, for we have now weighed and are proceeding south on the ebb . . .

We have been stuck fast on a bank in the Middle of the River these last 3 hours all because of the inattention of the man that was heaving the lead. There is no damage that we know of and the ship will float off on the flood. It is a reminder to me and to the officers that the men must constantly be watched over, many of them not having the sense to understand the dangers of a coast such as this. The need of a consort is very apparent in our loneliness and in an area where the constant sudden gales seem always to blow on-shore. And if both ships were driven on to the rocks I do not know what we should do.

It is constantly in my mind, the thought of wintering here in the manner of the early Hudsons Bay people. I do not think many would survive. There are forests here from which we could fashion some sort of boat, but as we proceed north I think the barrenness of the land, which is already to be seen in some of the rocky islands, will increase and the trees grow smaller until there is nothing to our purpose in the event of disaster.

I have been on many hostile coasts, but never on one that continued for such a great length. Constant vigil is our only safeguard, the which means little sleep and the danger of officers, not excluding myself, making wrong judgments and decisions through weariness.

The one gain as we go Northward is that the nights are already become very short. Soon there will be no darkness. But then the decision that I dread will be close upon me, for I am in command and whether to proceed or turn back will be for me to decide. I fear I am a man of too little imagination to have fully understood what a burden of responsibility for mens lives I was laying upon myself when I jumped to my feet at my Lord Sandwichs dinner party and said I would go upon this expedition. Pray God that when the time comes I am strong enough to make the right decision.

41

ALASKA AND
A RUSSIAN NOTE

Sunday, June 28th

Today we broke through to the Northward of that great archipelago of islands that the Russians discovered running so far to the Westward. We came through a Passage close by Oonalaschka Island, having a breeze at S and the tide with us; but the *Discovery* was not so fortunate, being carried back by the ebb into the race where the tide ran 6 knots. Even near the shore where we are now anchored it runs 5½.

We had a great deal of fog and mist this last month and 2 days ago, when we were off the NE shore of Oonalaschka, what I feared most did very nearly happen. The weather was so thick that we could scarce see the length of half a cable and hearing breakers on our starboard bow I had the anchor let go and called for the *Discovery* which was close by us to do the same.

When at length the fog cleared I perceived that we had sailed between two high rocks. I would not have ventured into those waters or anywhere near those rocks on a clear day, yet providence had guided us through in dense fog. I hope I may regard this as a good omen, but we were all of us a deal shaken by the sight of such dangers so narrowly missed and I am reminded once again that the fogs on this coast present the gravest danger, so that however much I desire to make the Northward with all speed, I must take the greatest care if we are to return to those we love.

A few days previous to this, when we had passed through a narrow Channell between the land and a group of rocks, the *Discovery* suddenly fired 3 guns. Fearing she had suffered some accident and sprung a leak I immediately sent a boat to her. It returned soon after with Capt Clerke who showed me a small thin wood case that was proffered him by an Indian in one of the several canoes which were following the Ship. This case opened in 2 halves and in it was a piece of paper with some writing which we took to be in the Russian language. There was nothing we could make of it except a date which was 1776. Capt Clerke thought it might be word from some Russian sailors ashore that had been shipwrecked, but in that case they would undoubtedly have come out to the ships themselves and I considered it to be a note of information left by a Russian trader for the advice of the next one of their ships that came this way. On my supposing this, and Capt Clerke finally agreeing it to be most likely, we had some comfort of it, that if our ships were destroyed and we marooned ashore there was some hope that we might be rescued by a vessel trading out of Russia.

All to the N of us is now open sea, which if the maps are to be believed will lead us direct to the Straits that Capt Behring discovered. Nevertheless, I intend to sail N Eastward along the N shore of these islands until I come up with the mainland coast again, so that I can map it and be sure there is no passage through it to the NE.

42

FOG
AND MORE FOG

Sunday, August 2nd

For a month past we have had calms and fogs, these last being at times so dense we could not see the length of the ship, so that progress has been slow and wearisome. But at least I have been able to correct some of the misapprehensions contained in Mr Stählins *Map of the New Northern Archipelago* in that the islands of his Archipelago run out continuous from a long narrow peninsular of the Mainland, rather in the manner of Mr Müllers map. But that is all of my achievement, there being no passage through this part of the Continent to the NE, though we had hopes that were proved false when we sailed into a wide river entrance just Northward of the Alaschka Peninsula.

This river I called the Bristol and a few days later, when we had so little wind it was only the strong tide that moved us, I sent Mr Williamson to climb an elevated promontory the better to see the form the coast took to the N of us.

There he took possession of the Country in the name of His Majesty, left a bottle with a piece of paper in it giving the name of the ships and the date, and returned on board with the information that the coast bore nearly N, also the country inland of it was without any tree or shrub, the hills naked and only the lower ground bearing any grass or other plants.

From this I conclude that we have progressed N of the tree line and shall find none hereafter, nor any shelter if we are driven upon the coast. Shortly after I last wrote anything here I was brought another piece of paper written upon in Russian and a young Indian who came aboard very wet after his canoe was upset put on dry cloathes I gave him with such ease I was assured that he was no stranger to our sort of apparel, so that by this and other signs it is clear the Russians come to this coast more often than was generally supposed. But I do not think they will have come N of the Alaschka peninsula and islands for there is nothing of trade to draw them to these coasts.

We are now in latitude 61°N with no sight of any passage so that I do not think any such exists south of Capt Behrings straits. So much slow wearisome toil in diligently searching this coast and all of it to no purpose other than to prove that what has been believed for so long is no more than the vague hopes of men who have let imagination run beyond the reality of it, as was the case with that Southern Continent.

Am I destined to return home again with nothing to show for this expedition but proof that a connection between the two great oceans of the Atlantic and the Pacific is no more than a dream? There will be no reward for me in that, nor any advancement. Men do not much favour their dreams being dashed to the ground; all I shall then have is my own satisfaction in the knowledge that I have pressed the matter to the limit and done what no man has done before, that is to map this coast in as much detail as the wretchedness of the weather with its fogs, calms and sudden gales has allowed.

Already I have abandoned the coast and am making up towards the straits. But I have little hope that the seas beyond will be open and free of any ice, for beyond the straits we shall be above 70° latitude N which is more than I ever sailed to the southward in the Southern Hemisphere without meeting up with ice floes.

Tuesday, August 4th

My Surgeon, Mr Anderson, having died yday, I have now had the *Discovery*s Surgeon, Mr Law, transferred to my own ship and discharged Mr Samwell into the *Discovery* to be surgeon there, he having been previously my Surgeons 1st mate. Mr Anderson who had been lingering under a consumption expired between 3 and 4 of the After noon and he being such a loss to us all, and particularly to me for his discourse and knowledge of natural history, I named the land we sighted to the Wward shortly after his death Andersons Island.

43

THROUGH THE STRAITS
AND INTO THE ICE

Monday, August 17th

We are now through the straits and in latitude 70°33′N. This position, together with our longitude of 197°41′E we got by some flying observations, both Sun and Moon shining out at intervals towards Noon. At the same time we perceived a brightness on the Northern horizon, which I think to be the blink that is reflected from large fields of ice. We hardly expected to meet ice so soon, but the weather has been very gloomy these last days and there is a sharpness in the air, so that I fear that it will prove to be ice that is ahead of us.

I have explored both shores of the Straits insofar as the weather permitted, naming the most Westerly extremity of all America hitherto known Cape Prince of Wales, and I have myself landed on an island on the Western side to see an Esqumaux village, the which together with the people and their weapons I have described in my Journal. They are very similar in all respects to those we have met with on the American coast. But what to make of the land we have seen beyond in comparison with the maps I have on board I do not know, the conditions of the weather making exact observations extremely difficult. I am inclining to the opinion that the maps are exceeding erroneous even to the latitude and have written thus in my Journal. If as I now begin to fear we are forced to come back this way I shall endeavour to make closer examination of this shore.

The two coasts in the Straits were distant from each other

some 7 leagues and when we returned to the American side the trend of the coast forced us in a NWesterly direction. We were leading for depth of water all the time and I had little or no sleep, not knowing what I might expect. Yesterday we came round to a more Easterly course, Fog and the Wind strong with it, which made it very dangerous, for the little we had seen of the land had shown it to be low, the which suggests there may be banks off it.

Since we are making steadily to the N Eastward I do believe that we are now upon the Top of the American Continent. My officers and others of the men who have also been excited by the thought that they may be the first to sail N from one Ocean to the other have been in great spirits since passing through the Straits and finding open water to the N.

If it is ice ahead, the disappointment will be very great. It is cold now and all of us are very tired who have the safety of the ships in their care.

Presuming that it is ice and we find there is a gap between it and the shore through which we may proceed, the decision whether to go on or turn back will be a very difficult one. I must not then through weariness or fatigue make a wrong decision, for in that lies the greatest danger. And I cannot sleep, for there is very little night and the safety of the ships my responsibility . . .

At 10 p.m.

It is ice. I was called up from the Cabbin about 1 p.m. with the information that a large field of it was sighted from the masthead. Shortly after I was on deck we could all see it and by ½ past 2 we were up to it, tacking close to it in 22 fathoms water, the latitude 70°41′N and the icefield extending from WbyS to EbyN and seemingly impenetrable. There being no way through to the Eastward I turned to the W. We had an abundance of Sea Horses* around the ship and I would have hoisted out the boats to improve our diet but that the wind freshened.

44

THE DECISION TO TURN BACK

Tuesday, August 18th

The Noon observation showed that we had gained nothing sailing to the Westward since our position is now 5 leagues further to the E than it was yesterday, the latitude being 70°44′N. We have 20 fathoms water and are close to the Ice which is 10 or 12 feet high and as compact as a Wall; further to the Northward it appears even higher though with pools of Water.

I turned S and after sailing 6 leagues found the Water shoaled to 7 fathoms. We were in this depth for ½ a league, after which it deepened very slightly. The haze, which had been thick, then cleared slightly so that we could see land 3 or 4 miles distant, all of it very low and much encumbered by ice, because of which I named it Icy Cape.

Sunday, August 30th

I have now been to the Westward as far as I may. Yday we were within 3 miles of the Asian shore with the depth of

* Walrus.

Water decreasing very fast to only 8 fathoms. We had no Noon observation, the weather being hazey with drizzling rain, but the previous Noon our latitude was 69°17'N so that we were to the southward of our furthest position on the American shore and all to the N great masses of ice.

Our spruce beer is finished and we have great need of Wood and Water. There is no Wood to be had here, the coast which trends in a Westerly direction being the same as the American shore, barren of everything but a sort of Moss.

I have informed the Ships company that I am now turning back for the Straits and that we will try again for the Passage next year. There was much relief at this, for the last 2 weeks have been very wearisome and full of peril to our safety, and though I took good care to warn them that everything on board must be considered of the most urgent necessity to our purpose, I fear they do not think ahead so far as a year, but consider only the moment and that we are turning Southwards.

My reason for turning back is chiefly that the Season is now too far advanced. Soon the sea will start to freeze again, which is one thing I have proved, that the sea does freeze, and freezes to a most terrible extent. I am also greatly concerned at the state of the ships, the rigging, sails and masts in particular, as well as the leaks. Navy ships are never put to such desperate hard work and their gear never intended to last so great a length of time. Everything is rotten and giving way, all except that which the Navy Yard condemned and the Boatswain with great good sense got back, the which is clear proof that *Resolution* was better fitted at Whitby for the coal trade than ever a Navy ship for battle.

One other matter that concerns me is that Mr Stählins Map shows 2 passages to the N between the American and

Asian continents, one either side of the great island of
Alaschka, and Behrings route through the Western passage.
When I turned back from my farthest N I thought Icy Cape
to be a part of the Mainland of America. I do not think I
was mistaken in this, but I intend to assure myself that it was
not a part of the N coast of Alaschka Island by further
examination of the American shore S of Cape Prince of
Wales.

If my view of the matter is correct, and there is no way
through to the N, then I must be sure to arrive at the Straits
at least 2 months sooner next year and endeavour to work
the Ships between the Ice and the American shore, so reaching Baffin Bay before the seas start to freeze again. From all
that I have perceived so far I fear this may prove a most
desperate venture, but since I am sent upon this Voyage for
one purpose only I intend with the help of Providence to
carry it to a successful end. I do but wish we had been more
fortunate this year, for another Winter spent in the islands
will contribute nothing to the good of either ships or men,
and if I stay the Winter upon the Asian side, it will be worse,
for we would be forced to lie idle at Petropaulowska in
Kamtschatka 6 or 7 months.

Sunday, September 13th

I have now cruzed down the Asian shore as far as the Straits,
and after passing through these and crossing to the American
side, we discovered a big Sound trending NE which gave me
hope that Stählins Map was right and there was another way
through to the north. When we were well into it, and still
hoping that the larboard shore might in truth be that island
of Alaschka, we came into shallow water with only 3½
fathom and the ship stirring up Mud from the bottom. I

called this Bay after Sir Fletcher Norton and the Sound also, my having no better opinion of either than others have of the man.

Sunday, September 20th

On Thursday last Mr King returned from the expedition into Norton Bay I had sent him upon. He confirmed there was no way through even for the boats, having discovered it to terminate in a small river about 3 or 4 leagues beyond where our ship nearly took the ground. So the Stählin Map is a fraud and Mr Müllers Map nearer to the truth.

45

THOUGHTS OF WINTER AND FAILING GEAR

Sunday, October 25th

Tomorrow I intend to depart from our anchorage here at Samgoonoodha, which is the same we were at on our voyage N. We have been here more than 3 weeks, which is scarce enough to do all that we had to do, which is to repair the leaks under the Sheathing where the seams were quite open and clear the Fish and Spirit rooms, also the after hold, and re-stow in such manner that if we suffer further leaks the water will find its way freely to the pumps. We have replenished the store of vegetables which we previously got here and are now decayed, and have taken on board plenty of fish, some including Salmon both fresh and dried we had from the Natives, but the most we caught ourselves with one Halibut that weighed 254 lb.

My greatest interest at this place was the meetings I had with the Russians who are resident here. They know nothing of the Continent of America to the North or of my Maps or of Lt Sindo, but have a great reverence for Capt Behring. Having set down all that they told me, more particularly my discourses with the chief among them, a Mr Ismyloff, in my Journal I will not repeat it here, except to say that the conclusion I have reached from my own observations does not vary greatly from the view expressed by Mr Ismyloff. This is that there being no tide nor any current to be discerned in the Straits and no hollow seas that I would expect with the Wind at N, the two Continents are either joined by land or ice, and the latter most likely having ourselves seen such a mass of it spread across a full 20° of longitude.

The information I got of Mr Ismyloff about the Kamtscha-tka coast, and also of Jacob Iwanowitch, another Russian who was Capt of a small vessel at Oomanak, together with the 2 charts I was shown, will relieve me of much anxiety when I fall in with that coast.

This is now my intention, to return to the Sandwich Islands for some of the Winter months, then to proceed to Kamtschatka to be at the harbour of Petropaulowska by the Middle of May. I shall give Capt Clerke these two objectives as our rendezvous in the event of the Ships become separated, and when we have purchased what we may urgently need of the Russians at Petropaulowska I shall make to the Nward with as much speed as the Weather allows and hope that Providence will be with us in the Year 1779 and lead us through into Baffin and Hudsons bays.

Meantime there is the Winter ahead of us, which offers nothing but months of wearisome waiting with all that it entails of labour to keep the ships in a sufficient state of readiness and the men reasonably content. Boredom I do know to be very destructive of that necessary determination and high spirit, so that discipline may not be enough and all my endeavours will again have to be directed to keeping my People fully occupied. And, wherever we are, constant guard will have to be kept against the thievery of the natives, for we have all too little now of those necessities on which the state of our vessels depend. This I find most irksome, since it depends so greatly upon myself and upon my standing with the island chiefs. Harsh measures may have to be taken, the which I do not like, since they are innocent of malice and their going off with whatever takes their fancy something quite as natural to them as the behaviour of children.

Sunday, November 8th

On the 30th of last Month we sailed through the pass between Oonalaschka and Oonalla and have since sailed S from the Archipelago as far as latitude 40°. The day before we made through the pass we sighted an elevated rock like a tower, the high seas nowhere breaking except against its shores, so that it must be very steep-to. Its appearance was a dreadful reminder of the dangers of sailing in waters that are not properly charted, for it is not marked on the Russian Map and we must have passed very near to it during the night.

Yesterday Capt Clerke came on board, there being little wind, to report the failure of more gear. On the night of the 2nd, when there was a Storm that blew very Violent and we heard the *Discovery* fire 3 times, it was apparently the Signal to bring to because of damage to sails and ropes. But much worse, the 2nd night after we left Samgoonoodha the Main tack gave way in a squal killing one man out right and wounding the Boatswain and some others.

This news was a most terrible reminder to me that there is a great deal of work to be done on the ships before they face the Ice again and if the Sandwich Islands, for which we are now headed, do not provide a sufficient shelter I do not know what I may do for the best. To go further south means a greater distance to sail when we turn north again, and if we were to encounter one of those great storms of which we had information in the Society Islands and again at Bolabola it is very doubtful that we could ride it out in the present state of the ships. I could wish that those men whose responsibility it was to fit our ships for sea were with us now. They would then learn what poor material and workmanship means in lives, discomfort and danger.

PART SIX

Hawaii:
Prelude to Disaster

46

A STUPID
MUTINOUS BEHAVIOUR

Thursday, November 26th, 1778

Land was sighted this morning at day breake, the which I take to be some part of the Sandwich Islands, though not any we know since we are now approaching these islands from E whereas when we discovered them in January we were to the S and W of them. The temperature is now over 80° which is a great change to our condition since but a month ago it was little above 40°. The relief I felt at our arrival was somewhat lessened by the nature of the shore which everywhere appeared steep to and rocky with a great sea breaking and a hill like a saddle disappearing into Clouds. Nowhere did I see any good bay or anchorage which was my most urgent need, though for days past both ships had been hard at work repairing sails, gear and boats.

At Noon we were close in to an isthmus that ran out from the heights, but though the land was low it was still rock bound. This was the more tiresome since I could see there was wood and water ashore, also people and plantations to supply our needs. Canoes now came off to us and the natives came into the ship without the least hesitation, all of them most friendly and of the same Nation we had met with when we were in this area before.

In the excitement of their arrival a black cat that was with us fell overboard, but instead of drowning, which some might have regarded as ill luck, it was brought back on board by one of the canoes which had picked it up about

2 miles astern of us.

I had already given orders that all men were to be examined for that disease which I am determined they shall not communicate to these islands. But on their coming on board I learned from the natives that they already had the disease and they spoke of it being past on to them by the people of Atowi where we had been before. However, I do know if there were Spaniards here before us we may not be the cause of their complaints; but I cannot be sure for the need of our People is such that whatever my orders and however strictly enforced they will always find some means of getting at the women and the women themselves ignorant of any sense of chastity are quite free with their charms.

I have also given strict orders that there is to be no trading other than through those appointed by me or Capt Clerke. I have already exchanged Nails and pieces of iron for Cuttle fish and am informed there is plenty of fruit and roots ashore, also hogs and fowls, and these they will bring off tomorrow so that we shall have the benefits of fresh provisions to our diet, which recently has been none of the best.

One thing I can say for this place, the natives appear more honest than anywhere I have been in the Pacific Ocean, not one of them making any attempt to steal from us.

Sunday, November 29th

We have had much difficulty with women here. They come out to trade their bodies and when sent away they turn quite nasty as though it was a slight upon their charms when it is only for their own and their peoples good, and so that we shall not be accused later of carrying the disease. We did a good trade on Friday getting of them bread fruit, potatoes, tarra roots, a few plantains and pigs for which they seemed satisfied with nails and pieces of iron which is about all we have left to trade with. Our decks were quite crowded with them and when the trading was done they were dancing and singing for us, everyone seeming happy.

The land to the Westward of us appeared to be another island and since we were drifting to windward though lying to I decided to ply to windward and so get round the E side of the island into its lee, the seas here being very big.

Now that I am back in warmer climate with the prospect of re-fitting the ships and another attempt to find a way through to the Atlantic next year, I find my mind dwelling upon the time spent on that fog bound coast and in close proximity to the northern ice with something that is near foreboding, knowing how fortunate we are to have got S again without damage to our ships or any disaster. I fear the long hours on constant watch for real and imagined dangers have tired me more than I dare admit even to myself, for I never felt like this before. It is something I cannot communicate to any living soul, not even to Capt Clerke, who being sick is in less condition than myself to face the perils of another season in the north.

I have constantly now to keep a hold on my temper for I am at times very irritable, the smallest matters upsetting me most. The keeping of my official Journal has become a wearisome business, not being able to write what I do in truth feel since those who would read it in the safe security of the Admiralty Office would not understand, they never having spent years at sea in total isolation from their fellows nor carried upon their shoulders the weight of responsibility for an expedition engaged for so long in such hazardous exploration. Only here can I express my thoughts freely and these are of the most gloomy, for there is the Winter before me, the same endless routine keeping men and ships in condition, and ultimately the ice again and the constant watch as we search for a passage I no longer believe exists. But it must be done if I am to report on my return that there is no such passage, the which they will not accept, and blame me accordingly, unless I can prove to the satisfaction of my officers and all who keep their own Journals on board that we have pressed the search with so much diligence and determination that nobody, however hostile to me personally, can doubt the truth of it.

When I was in England there was some curiosity expressed as to my state of mind sailing in seas where no man had been before and charting the shores of unknown lands. Even my Lord Sandwich asked me once was I never afraid? In such circumstances no man but a fool is a stranger to fear. But all I said was, not that I was aware of. And this was the gist of the reply I gave to all that asked me, the which they accepted as the proper reply of a naval officer and the truth too since it is my nature to appear unemotional. But it is not the truth, nor ever can be, for a man who knows exactly the risks he is taking, and because he is the commander, and by his direction putting all the men that sail with him at similar risk, the fear of what may happen is something he has to live with day and night.

And particularly at night, for on deck or at work in the cabin the mind is occupied with the active details of navigation and mapping. But in the night imagination is free to consider all desperate possibilities, which I do believe to be some necessary preparation of the mind for the instant action that must be taken in the event of some disaster overtaking one or other of the ships. I did not sleep much during the long period we were off the American coast, and now that the nights are so much longer and myself less extended, I have more time to indulge myself, yet sleep does not come readily as it used to. My chief concern at the

present is that the coast of these islands we are come upon is
hostile in the extreme and the seas very big, so that I fear
I must wait upon a change in the weather before we can
come to a satisfactory anchorage.

Wednesday, December 2nd

Something no one of us had expected so far S as Lat. 20°,
the mountains of this larger island which we have stood off
and on from all night are covered in snow, some of it appearing deep and to have laid there some time. The island we
were previously off is called Mow'ee and this one O'why'he.*
The wind remains at SE and while still off the NE end of the
former island we received a visit from the Chief of these
parts, who is called Terreeoboo. The natives of O'why'he
are for some reason very shy of us, but in the end we were
able to persuade them to bring off all that we needed and
our trading with them did not cease until it was getting
dark. I am now plying to windward again with the intention
of rounding the island and shall soon be much occupied with
Mr King in preparing for Fridays eclipse of the Moon.

Friday, December 4th

By the Eclipse just observed the mean longitude was 204°
35'. On reducing all observations to the Timekeeper at 4h30'
it was 204°04'45"E.

Monday, December 7th

I can scarcely control my temper for the behaviour of the
men, and also the apparent loss of the current we had previously observed setting us to windward. Of the behaviour

* Cook's phonetic spelling of Hawaii.

of the men in refusing even to taste the sugar cane beer I
have had brewed in order to save our Spirits I have written
at some length in my Journal, for it is not to be borne, and
my Lords and the Publick must understand that my insistence on their drinking home brewed beer is for their own
good and to save their Grog, the which is now very precious,
there being so little of it remaining, and that their behaviour
has become close to mutinous and my anger at it wholly
justified.

But though I can discipline the men, I cannot discipline
the wind or currents, so that though we ply constantly to
windward we make little progress, the which is an aggravation to the men who have little in their minds but to get
on shore where I know they will make free with the women
and following upon that they will begin to desert as happened
before.

We have three months at least to wait until we begin to
work N again along the Russian coast of Kamtschatka, and
if there is to be such thoughtless mutinous behaviour this
early in the Winter it is evident I cannot indulge them, but
must speak out to the assembled men and enforce my will
with the most strict discipline.

Added to this annoyance and the contrariness of the weather, the ship is leaking, and not as before from the upper
works, but from her bottom. If it opens up worse we may
have to attempt a fothering such as we did after hauling
the *Endeavour* off the reef.

Sunday, December 13th

Still plying to windward off the NE coast of O'why'he,
regularly coming in to trade with the natives. Today we stood
in again, but had only made 6 leagues to windward, so that
I and all on board begin to tire of our continued beating and

fear some devil is at work to prevent our turning the End of the island, so enabling us to work round into the lee. Nowhere in the Tropicks have I met so high or so troublesome a sea as we have had these last weeks on the E side of these islands, and though the direction of the wind shows frequent shifts of 4 or more points, allowing us some progress, there is never any reduction of the sea, which makes living on board exceeding unpleasant. And if it adds to my temper, I can sometimes understand how the men feel, deprived of the promise of terra firma and the hope of women after being so long upon the desolate shores of North America.

But though I can understand their mood, I cannot, and dare not, condone it or in any way indicate sympathy with it. The stupid mutinous behaviour they showed in refusing the sugar cane beer we brewed, which had hops in it to give it some sharpness and flavour, was followed later by their delivering to me a most impudent letter. In this they did not only declare their refusal to touch the decoction because they did not like it, but complained of the scanty provisions I was allowing them. This was not to be borne with since the allowance of provisions was that commonly served while the ship was among the islands of the Pacific. However, I was more concerned to save us our Spirits for the colder climate N of Alashka and so had all hands mustered aft, when I spoke to them fayre on the matter of the allowance, telling them it was the first I heard of it being in any way scanty and that they should have more allowed to them if that was what they wished. But on the matter of Grog, I told them bluntly they would get none at all other than they drank the cane decoction every other day. And on they declaring the brew to be unwholesome and injurious to health, despite the fact that they had last year in the islands been stealing sugar cane from the plantations at any opportunity and eating it raw, I said it was nothing of the kind and if they would not drink it then I would have the Brandy Cask struck down into the hold and they can make do with water and nothing else.

I gave them 24 hours to consider my offer, and when they would have none of it, refusing absolutely to drink of the decoction, I kept my word and had the Brandy Cask sent down. That was not the end of it, Wm Griffiths, a cooper, taking the matter into his own hands and starting the cask in which was the cane beer so that it went sour. He was punished yday with 12 lashes and I took the opportunity of the crew being assembled to speak to them again about the stupid and mutinous nature of their behaviour.

This, and the desertions that I know will be attempted when we finally come to an anchorage and the time draws near for the ships to head N again, causes me constantly to consider how best I can deal with the men, it being a fine point how much they must be forced and how much indulged. The *Resolution* and *Discovery* are both Navy ships and the officers and men in them subject to Naval discipline, but in voyages of discovery of the length of 3 years the enforcement of discipline is not something that can be taken as granted, being dependant on the acceptance of it by all, not as of right but for the greater good of everybody. This is most particularly so at the mid point of the voyage, the which we are now at, for it is then that all, myself and my officers included, are feeling the greatest degree of weariness, our homes still perhaps eighteen months away and more hardships and dangers ahead of us before we may turn the ships heads for England.

No mention of these doubts and concerns of mine can be made in my Journal, the which makes it tiresome to work over, and the Publick when they read it will have a very false impression, all seeming so much more simple and straightforward than it really is.

Facing the assembled men yday after Griffiths had been flogged and understanding their mood very well from the time I had spent in the Navy as a seaman, I felt very much alone, conscious that the custom of obedience and my own demeanour was but a very thin wall to the dam of their feelings bursting and a mutiny breaking out. There was no reasoning with them and no logic in the faces I looked down upon. This was evidenced by their total rejection of the beer I had had brewed, though 12 months since all had accepted the spruce decoction with evident enjoyment, and also by their being incapable of looking to the future and how they would manage on the edge of the ice with no Spirits to warm their bellies, which was again very different to last year when they had so readily accepted that the Grog should be saved for when we were in colder climates.

This wretched big sea and the Wind always in the same quarter is the chief cause of their complaint. I cannot expect them to understand that I must continue to make to windward when even my officers find some difficulty, only Capt Clerke really seeming to understand that if we turn downwind we shall probably never regain our position. It is very essential to our safety that we are not blown from these islands where, once we can round the E point of O'why'he, we shall have a lee and smoother water, also the prospect of some suitable anchorage for repairs. This we are in increasing need of, the leak in our bottom so bad that water has got into the Gunners store room making it necessary yday to try and stop it with oukum in a net drawn down by ropes in the hope that the pressure of water entering the hull would force the fothering to hold.

47

YARD OFFICERS
CONDEMNED

Sunday, December 20th

Yesterday we came very near to weathering the island, which the natives have confirmed to me as the most windward of the group. We also came near to being set on shore, for after a week of variable winds in which it sometimes blew hard in squals, and at other times fell calm with thunder lightning and rain, it suddenly fell quite Calm. This was at one o'clock in the morning with a big NEasterly swell which set us down so fast upon the land that though we were at first some 5 leagues off, we were very soon barely a league from the shore and could see lights. Again the calm was accompanied by thunder lightning and rain, the night being very dark.

To our great relief a breeze then came in from SE by E, but then we had squals with rain and were in some peril when the Main topsail leach gave and the sail rent in two, and then the 2 topgallant sails went the same way. At day breake we saw we were off the E point of the island at last and everywhere a dreadful surf breaking.

I fear that what I wrote in my Journal about the failure of the sails, I being very angry at the time, may have to be reconsidered. But the blame does lie with the Navy yard*

* Sir Hugh Palliser, Comptroller of the Navy, who was responsible for the Navy yards, proved very touchy about Cook's reference to this in his official Journal and requested Dr Douglas to suppress it in the book, pleading somewhat speciously that

for the bolt-ropes are not equal to the strength of the sails. Indeed, what I have said is that nothing of the Navy's gear is the equal of that in general use by the Merchant service and the Yard officers seem to have had no consideration for the time their gear would be required to stand up, though they knew very well we would be away upwards of 3 years. It makes me very angry to think upon it, that for lack of consideration or any imagination these men ashore set my ships and the lives of my men at risk. Again I do wish they were on board to stand with me and see the surf breaking upon the rock shores of this mountainous island. Did they thus know what a danger they put us to they would quake in their shoes and their conscience be overcome at the risk to their own lives. But the men who order the gear and rig our ships never sail in them, which is something I greatly regret, wishing with all my heart that I had them with me, not only here but in the far N among the ice fields.

Sunday, December 27th

Another Christmas is gone and I barely noticed it, except to say a prayer for my family at home and think briefly of their celebrating it again without me. My concern is for the *Discovery* which we lost sight of on Thursday morning.

Cook did not know what he was talking about – 'It would need a long Note to explain Capt. Cooks Error it being out of his line.'

48

AN ANCHORAGE
AT LAST

Sunday, January 3rd, 1779

A very hard rain ushered in the New Year. But we are finally round the E point of the island, still plying and trading when close to the shore. Some of the hog bought I have salted for use when we are upon coasts where none is available. The natives are hard bargainers and maintain the price of their provisions even when they bring off more than we need, being quite prepared to take all back to the shore again whatever the difficulties of landing. I never could persuade them to bring off sufficient only for our immediate requirements. Either they brought too much or too little, and if we purchased more than our requirements the nature of the roots and fruits is such that in the temperature prevailing they instantly rot, something that the men through perverseness refused to comprehend so that they imagined they were justified in their complaint that they had too little allowance of fresh provisions, which on some days was undoubtedly the case.

Sunday, January 10th

Today the Wind has veered, the easterlies giving way to light airs from NW and SW, finally blowing fresh from WNW with rain. We are now off the SW shore of the island, having passed the S point of it on Tuesday where we could see a large village. The following day I sent Mr Bligh away in a boat to sound the coast with orders to land and look for fresh water. His report was far from encouraging, he finding no bottom with a 160 fathom of line as close as 2 cables from the shore and on land only rainwater in rock pools made brackish with sea spray and the country composed of large slags and ashes partly covered with plants.

I am at something of a loss now where to go for an anchorage, the island being much broken up and half destroyed by volcanic disturbance, so devastated in fact that it is a matter for wonder where the natives grow all the abundance of fruit and vegetables they bring off to us. Can the mountain that is covered with snow be the Volcano that has caused all this devastation? It does not appear like any I have seen before, yet the destruction that is everywhere visible to the naked eye must have occurred not very long ago.

There is a strong current setting SE and the only good thing that has happened this past Week is that the *Discovery* has rejoined us. This she did at 1 p.m. on Thursday, 7th January, Capt Clerke coming on board and informing me that after we parted he plied round the E part of the island, but then had unfavourable winds and was carried some distance off the coast, all the time with one of the islanders on board who had remained there at his own choice.

It is a great relief to have Capt Clerke with me again, for I am heartily sick of standing off and on this wretched island not knowing what best to do. But though we discussed the matter of an anchorage he had no other information to offer and so we reached no conclusion. This lack of any prospect that would make a decision possible is having a very bad effect upon me personally and upon everyone on board of the ship.

Sunday, January 17th

We have been up to the NW of the island, the weather being sometimes Calm, sometimes fresh gales. On the night of the 13th the Wind veered westward and by morning we had been set back all we had gained. Yday, when plying to the northward again and within 3 leagues of the coast, I sighted what looked like a bay and sent Mr Bligh in with a boat from each ship to look at it Shortly after he had left, about 10 o'clock, we had the most extraordinary sight, our 2 ships being quite surrounded by a dense mass of canoes filled with all manner of produce so that it must have been gathered from every part of the island. I think there were not less than one thousand canoes massed about the ships.

Today it has been the same. At first we counted 500 canoes about the *Resolution* and another 300 around the *Discovery*. By the afternoon so many had joined them that we quite lost count. Mr King reckoned at least 1500 and with a generality of 6 natives to each, the population around us was something close to 10,000 allowing that women and young boys were swimming off to us from the shore. They were like a shoal of fish in the sea about us, even men on pieces of wood. This is the greatest number of natives I have seen assembled in one place in the whole Pacific Sea, the shore at times being quite thick with them. And all unarmed. The women also very bold.

This was after we had at last come to anchor, which we did at 11 a.m. in 13 fathom a quarter of a mile off shore, the bottom sandy. We then immediately unbent the sail and struck yards and topmasts, hoping our anchors would hold us if it came on to blow from SW. This bay is called by the natives Karakakooa*.

* Kealakekua Bay.

Unfortunately the people on this side of the island are different from those on the N, they being as thieving as any we have met with, to the extent even that some of those that are swimming about the ship have equipped themselves with a stone headed stick for use as a tool to extract the nails out of the sheathing under water. And their desire to stay the night on board is not for the sake of curiosity but what they might take in the darkness.

However, this appears a very disciplined and organised society in that they accord their priests and their chiefs absolute obedience. One of the latter, a man called Parea, who said he was a servant of King Terreeoboo, when I appealed to him instantly drove them all off the ship. Before this I had observed the *Discovery* with so many clinging like flies to one side of her that she was actually heeled over, because of which and the difficulty they were having to keep more from entering the ship, I sent the Chief Parea to get them off her.

49

TREATED AS A GOD

The chief priest of the place came to me with a piece of red cloth, which he wraped round me, also a large hog, two cocoanuts and some fruit. All the people of Note introduced themselves in similar manner. Then Touahah the Priest and Parea invited me to go on shore with them, the which I did accompanied by Mr King and Mr Bayly, and as soon as we landed we were conducted to a large *Morai*, which was the sacred place of one of their gods. This was after I had entertained Touahah, Parea and 2 other chiefs, Kaneina and Koah, to dinner. Here Koah, and a grave young man with a long beard called Kaireekea, took me by the hand and led me to the top of a Scaffold that was somewhat ricketty and had at the foot 12 images and offerings of a hog and fruit much rotted, and all the time muttering a prayer. Also in the village where we had been before coming to this sacred place everybody prostrated themselves at the sight of me as they had done before at the island of Atowee to the Westward.

There was now a sort of ceremony, some 10 men in procession and again this business of the Red Cloth, they all prostrating themselves before me, then handing the Cloth to Kaireekea who carried it to Koah and he wraped it round me and afterward gave me the hog they had brought, and all the time prayers being said in constant repetition. I was finally brought down off the Scaffold and taken to each of the images where words were said that appeared derogatory, except only to the Centre Image which was about 3 feet high and was the only one wraped in a Cloth. Before this image they fell prostrate and desired me to do the same, the which I did, the image being called Koonooakeea.

The Ceremony continued with another procession bearing gifts and a great repetition of prayers and the crowd constantly repeating Erono, Erono. A chewed cocoanut was then wraped in a cloth and rubbed all over me including the face and after that we were invited to eat, something I found difficult being handed the food by Koah and remembering that in the first ceremony he had been fondling a hog that was quite putrid while repeating the prayers. Seeing my difficulty the old man went so far as to chew it for me first so that I was glad finally to excuse myself by making a small speech and handing round gifts of iron and nails.

We left then, 2 men with wands going before and repeating again and again the word Erono and at the sound of it everybody prostrating themselves. What can this mean? That I am viewed as some sort of god? Is it their desire to propitiate me for this reason, or would they do this with anyone who came with the might of two ships and armed with cannons? I do not know and can only accept it as the work of Providence, it being so much to my purpose, and am resolved to play the part I am assigned to. For there is a proper social and religious structure in their society that enables discipline to be maintained so that orders when given are obeyed by all the people, and whether I am regarded as a God or a Chief does not concern me very much so long as they bring us what we need.

50

KING TERREEOBOO AND CEREMONIALS

Sunday, January 24th

We got our Observatory and Tents ashore the day after we anchored, choosing a field of Sweet Potatoes close beside the *Morai*, which at my request the priests then tabooed. Nevertheless I put a guard upon it of six Marines and a Corporal under their officer with orders to wear Regimentals on duty, which always ensures a certain respect, and not to allow the natives to handle their Muskets. This was not necessary for the taboo was so strictly enforced that no Women would come near whatever the inducement for fear, I was told, that either God or the King would kill them. It is for this reason that these people are the most amenable we have met with, that is so long as we hold the respect of the Chiefs and Capt Clerke and I continue to represent whatever it is we do to the priests. For this purpose, whenever I go ashore, I permit myself to be supported under the arms as is their wont and to go through the same ceremony of the priests singing and chanting some words and all prostrating themselves before me.

Parea was generally on hand when I came ashore and I understand that it is to the Chief Priest whose name is Kao and who will come with King Terreeoboo that I am indebted for all the presents of hogs and fruit and roots. Parea was often very hard on his own people, which is no doubt the reason they obey their Chiefs without question. The first day, or the day after, I cannot recall which a native who had stole something out of the *Discovery* was discovered by Parea, whereupon the man jumped overboard and the Chief after him. They were both under water a long time and when finally Parea alone came up half drowned he said the thief was dead, presumably throttled and most probably held down by one who undoubtedly had greater under water prowess.

Discipline seems better among the natives than among my own People. My orders to prevent the spread of the Venereal are more honoured in the breech, if that be not a rude way of putting it. I blame the women flaunting themselves and thus making contact between my men and themselves so easy, and if it is done too blatant and the man has not been cleared by Mr Samwell then I must discipline him. So tomorrow I will have 4 men flogged, Bradley with 2 dozen lashes for intercourse when he knew that he had the disease, the others 1 doz each for absenting themselves or for disobedience. I fear I may have more of this before I leave. Why cannot men perceive that orders are not given but for the good of all? Instead they give rein to their natural desires without thought for the future or for others and without the slightest degree of common sense.

Today there is peace round the ships. It seems that a taboo has been placed upon us, the natives being kept in their villages and no canoes allowed to put out. All this I believe because Terreeoboo is on his way to visit us, he being held in great awe and the same man that came on board of us off Mowee who I thought then to be just an ordinary Chief. This second meeting will be of more interest since I now know in what great awe he is held by people and understand very well that the manner of his signalling his coming is to impress me. How he will behave toward me will perhaps give me some clearer idea of how I am regarded by his people, whether as some god or emissary of a god or simply as the Commander of ships representing a powerful King across the ocean.

Monday, January 25th

The King has just left, it being after 10 at night and he having come on board in great state accompanied by an endless concourse of canoes.

I had been informed of his imminent arrival shortly after the disciplining of the men aforementioned and after I had been forced to order a Musket to be fired over a Chiefs head to make him desist from driving off the few canoes with which we were endeavouring to trade for much needed provisions. Towards evening a long line of canoes came round the N point of the Bay and I understand more were still coming in until it was too dark to see.

Terreeoboo treated me with the greatest respect and was accompanied by Kao who I think to be the High Priest of these parts.

Tuesday, January 26th

King Terreeoboo came out again today about Noon in great State but did not come on board. He had with him a canoe with 4 images and the priest called Kao, and another filled with hogs and vegetables for gifts, and the priests that were with Kao, if they were such, kept up a solemn chant. The images were of basket work and covered with feathers of red, black, white and yellow, with strangely distorted mouths full of dogs teeth and eyes of Pearl Oyster shell, and the Chiefs that were with the King resplendent in feather cloaks and caps.

After paddling round the ship the 3 canoes headed for the Observatory. I immediately followed in the pinace and was glad to see that Mr King had the Marines drawn up as a guard of honour. I met Terreeoboo in the Markee and at my entrance he rose and threw over me the very cloak he was wearing, placed a feathered cap on my head and handed me a feather-crowned fly-flap which I take to be a symbol of power. Afterward, when we had renewed our friendship, there came a procession of priests headed by the emaciated figure of Kao who wrapt a piece of cloth round me as before and presented me with a pig. After the usual religious chanting, everybody joining in the responses, I took the King and as many others as the pinace would hold back to the *Resolution* where I gave them all presents, some beads and iron things that I knew they valued.

In so many islands I have had to behave in such fashion that I now find it a wearisome business, their customs always of such serious formality though at other times they appear like children. But here the formality and discipline is very great and I cannot be sure if the real power is with the King or the Priests. And if I am regarded as some sort of a god, a

god called Lono or Erono, then is this because Terreeoboo
has declared it so, because I have power greater than his and
by making me a god my power does not detract from his
in the eyes of his people, or is it to the Priests with their
chants and cloth wraping ceremony that I owe my elevation?

Sunday, January 31st

Yesterday the Rudder was finished and sent on board, and
today I have sent the Carpenters into the Country to cut
timber for the head rail. Every time I go ashore the natives
prostrate themselves as they did for Terreeoboo and the
Priests. Kao, who lives in some religious houses close by
where we have the Observatory, is always there to greet
me with gifts, given with the usual Ceremony. But god or
not it does not discourage these people from thieving and it
is the Chiefs who are at the back of it. A box of knives,
forks and pewter plates has been taken from the Markee
though Mr King was sleeping there and a Marine centry on
guard. Capt Clerke has ordered a native flogged for stealing
and this morning Mr King tells me he was astonished to
have one of the greatest Chiefs come to him with gifts and
tied to his wrist was our Gunroom carving knife. He had
much difficulty persuading him it was not his property.

I shall be glad when all is repaired and we are at sea again,
free of the constant ceremonial, the thieving, and the temp-
tations of women. My greatest fear, which was desertions,
has not been realised, but I believe this is only because the
men know that the Chiefs and Priests have such power over
the people that they will be returned immediately. The
matter of provisions also causes me concern. My Gunner
and Mr Vancouver from the *Discovery* headed a party to the
interior of the Country to botanise, and also with the intention of reaching the top of the Snowy Mountain. They

report the land very difficult and full of the crumbling remains of Volcanic action, so that I begin to wonder how long the natives can continue to trade with us, the area of land they have for plantation being so circumscribed by slag and ash. Already I have been approached by some of the Chiefs to enquire when we will depart. I believe them to begin to resent our taking so much of their provisions even though we do always trade fairly with them.

Thursday, February 4th

We are now at sea again having weighed and sailed out from Karakakooa Bay early this Morning.

We made our farewells yday, I accompanied by King Terreeoboo going to the abode of the High Priest Kao where parcels of cloth and a vast quantity of red and yellow feathers was laid out, and beside this a great number of hatchets and other iron pieces which was our contribution. All this was for the King who then selected a goodly portion and offered it to me. I took but a small amount to show my appreciation so that the many hogs and other provisions were given to the Common People of the village. We took away in the boats a few of the largest hogs and only as much of the bread fruit and sweet potatoes as we could eat since they would not keep.

The priest Kao seems to have taken a great fancy to Mr King, who was my only companion on this occasion, for both he and Terreeoboo asked me to leave him on the island. Apparently they took Mr King for my son so that I had to excuse my taking him with me on the ground that I could not spare him, but would consider the matter again when I returned next year. He told me afterward that they had already pressed him to elope, promising to hide him in the hills till the Ships had sailed. I suppose I must take this as a compliment, but poor King was not a little put out at the time having to explain it all to me.

We had already got the Observatory and tents on board that morning and in the evening were entertained with boxing and wrestling, which was followed by the letting off of the rest of our fireworks.

The Wind is light, but we are now clear of the Bay and before it wax dark could see Mowee, which I intend to visit from the western side, and afterward we will map the rest of this island archepelago and get what provisions we can before heading for the Russian coast. There will be opportunity enough then to work on my Journal, something I seem not to have had either the time or the stomach for these past few weeks for I see that my last entry in it was foɪ 6th January.

Sunday, February 7th

Mr Bligh has returned safely with the pinace, which is a great relief as we have had such heavy squals from off the Snowy Mountain which is distant from us barely 5 or 6 miles that I was forced to furl the sails and bring to under Mizzin staysail. I had sent him away yday to explore the bay we are now off in hope of water, a native who was on board at his own insistence and who called himself Brittanee having said there was a good supply of it there and also shelter. But the Master reports nothing to our purpose, neither shelter nor water, and the native has stayed ashore. I think Mr Bligh may have upbraided him very severely for so misleading us.

On his way back to us, when he had a fayre wind, Mr Bligh was able to save an old woman and 2 men who had their canoe overturned in a squal while trying to get ashore. There were other canoes about but they offered no assistance.

It was not possible to save their canoe. The severe weather came on yday so that many canoes that had put out to us as they had done the previous day were forced to turn back. As a result of the suddenness of the tempest we have a number of women stranded on board so that the ship is somewhat overcrowded. It is this constant traffick with the natives and the sense of their being always about us crowding in upon us that makes life in these islands so very restless. It is hardly surprising that I get so little writing done.

Tuesday, February 9th

Yday Evening it came on to blow very fresh so that we reefed and got the Topgallant yards down and by Midnight it was Strong Gale. This morning at 6 it was reported to me that the head of the Foremast was sprung. It was still blowing very strong, but moderated toward Noon and I then had a full report of the damage. It appears that the mast is sprung at the point where we fished it in King Georges Sound, the fishes being made out of driftwood which the Carpenters did not much like at the time. The cause of its springing is undoubtedly the slack in the Fore topmast rigging which I had commented upon on our leaving Karakakooa Bay.

The question now is whether to continue in the hope that we may find suitable anchorage in some suitable bay in the islands we have not visited or return to that we know of? I fear it must be the latter, for to continue in our present state is too great a risk, and yet I am most reluctant to put back having taken our departure of those people who will again have to supply us while we make repairs. It was perhaps unfortunate that just before we sailed William Watman, who had been 21 years a Marine and one of the Gunners crew, died of some sort of Paralytic stroke. If I put back some of the men are sure to comment on this, believing such is their superstitious nature that the ghost of poor Watman has called us back, and he buried at the *Morai* by request of Kao and his priests.

Wednesday, February 10th

Last night I finally gave the order to bear away for Kara-kakooa, a decision I arrived at with the greatest reluctance. But perhaps it is better that the mast should have gone now rather than later on when we may be upon an even more hostile shore. The wind being now light and variable some canoes have come off to us enabling us to rid ourselves of the natives that were stranded on board by the bad weather.

Friday, February 12th

This morning at daylight we were anchored in 24 fathoms in Karakakooa Bay and very sorry I was to see the place again as also was the Ships company knowing there was much hard work ahead of them and my orders that no-one was to go on shore save he had orders to do so. By night fall Fore and Main topmasts were down and prepared as Sheers for getting the Foremast out of her. We will need to have Carpenters and Sailmakers ashore and Marines to guard their tools from thieving, all the difficulties we had before and more besides since I do fear we have ate out this part of the island of most available provisions. Very few canoes have come out to us and nobody seems rejoiced that we have returned.

51
TROUBLE BREWING

Saturday, February 13th

Entertained King Terreeoboo on board this morning, he and some of his Chiefs being as I feared much displeased at seeing us returned and very searching in their questions, though they can see very well the reason, the mast being ashore and all the Carpenters working on it. The foot of it is rotten as I saw when it was stepped, but it will have to do. I wish the Yard officers were here that they could see how the failure of their work endangers us at the hands of these people and the elements. I shall make a very full report to their Lordships, but by then we may have lost the ship as a result of the ill equipping of us for a voyage of this nature and duration.

After the King had been we had a great number of canoes about the ships, which had been tabooed until he had been on board. But they now insist on pieces of iron about 2 feet long for trade, like the 2 I gave to the King, I suppose for the purpose of hammering into daggers which they call *pahooahs*, and though we now have hogs and other provisions aplenty, with the canoes and the people comes thievery. This appears worse than it was before, the chiefest impudence occurred this morning when the Armourers Tongs on board of the *Discovery* was stolen. Capt Clerke had the native that did it seized and given 40 lashes, then strung up to the main shrouds till such time as the Tongs may be returned. There was more trouble in this connection this Afternoon, and to my mind much more serious since it involved one of the Chiefs.

It was reported to me by Mr King on my going ashore

that this man had made trouble with the natives who were employed and had been paid for assisting in the filling of the casks with water from the well at the far end of the beach. Mr Hollamby, recently appointed Quartermaster in the *Discovery*, who is in charge of the work, had requested a Marine whom Mr King sent back with him but only equipped with side arms, which was not sensible since by then the natives had armed themselves with stones. It was not until Mr King had spoken with the Chiefs, he being accompanied by another Marine armed with a Musket, was the work able to be continued without hindrance.

No sooner was I informed of this and myself engaged in inspecting the work of the Carpenters than there was Musket fire from the *Discovery* directed at a canoe which was being paddled towards the shore. I immediately set off along the beach to intercept it in company with Mr King and one of the Marines. There was a great crowd of people gathered and a good deal of noise, and though they gave back whenever the Marine presented his Musket, I noticed there was also laughter at the threat, and I do believe that the name Erono was more potent than the Musket, for mention of it caused the crowd to fly back some distance from me.

We proceeded in pursuit of the canoe until it was almost dark and then, being some 3 miles from the tents, we were led back by another route that was further from the sea than we had come by, and I believe this to have been done with intent, for when we returned to the Markee we were informed by the Coxswain of the Pinace of a more serious outbreak of violence against us. The pinace having gone to assist the *Discovery*s boat that was in pursuit of the canoe, on reaching the shore the chief Parea had roused the people against those that were in the pinace and they having no arms with which to defend themselves all the oars got broke and our men thoroughly beaten.

I was very angry at the Coxswains stupidity in going unarmed in pursuit when there was such an immense crowd of natives gathered and all showing signs of hostility, and he knowing very well that I had given orders before setting off in pursuit myself that the Marines were to fire if there was any more hostility against us.

The whole troublesome affair was due to the Tongs and the lid of a cask that contained salt horse, both being handed over to another canoe which returned them to the *Discovery*s Master who was in pursuit. There followed a most unfortunate misunderstanding, the Coxswain of the pinace thinking to capture the canoe that had made off with the Tongs and the natives that had stolen them leaping overboard and swimming ashore. Mr Vancouver got into the empty canoe and was just starting to paddle off with it to the *Discovery* when Parea, whose canoe it was and who was going ashore to recover that which had been stolen from us, got hold of it and hauled it back on shore, taking hold of the paddles so that the canoe could not be taken off to the ship, he fearing for the loss of it. Whereupon Mr Edgar tried to wrench it out of his hand, but being not so strong as Parea was pinned down. On assistance being sent, Parea let go and ran away, but towards the pinace, where he was struck by an oar wielded by one of our men.

This as far as I can learn from those that were involved was the true cause of this most unfortunate affray, the which has taken me some time of patient enquiry to unravel. It was Parea who made the mob desist, but on his going to get back the oars that had been taken, the crowd knocked Mr Vancouver down and would have stripped him of his cloathes and also got the ring bolts out of the pinace if Parea had not returned in time to stop them.

All this confusion is as much the fault of our people as

of the islanders and I fear it may not end there, for Parea went off in his canoe to the Town of Kowrooa where the King resides and has said he will come on board of the *Resolution* tomorrow doubtless to lay complaints before me. I have ordered all the Women out of the ship and told Mr King to have his centries keep a close watch ashore on the tents tonight and to open fire in the event any native attempts to creep up on them in the dark.

Tomorrow I will use my best endeavours to satisfy Parea for he is the one Chief who has at all times been at great pains to help us and I am very much disturbed by the rash behaviour of our People, fearing it may have antagonised him.

The generality of Chiefs is no longer friendly towards us and it is now my belief that only the Priests and the standing I have as some sort of a god that prevents the great mass of the people from arming themselves with their weapons and attacking us. This, and the use of our firearms, is I think sufficient to hold them in subjection for the time that it is necessary to complete the repairs to the mast and ship it. But from this moment forth a bold front is become necessary and in the event of more trouble I shall seize upon the person of the King himself and hold him until we sail, the situation being I fear more dangerous than it has ever been, so that I have no alternative but to employ force. And this largely because the officers and men act without thinking and do not seem to understand that once raised to a frenzy the numbers of these people is so vast and their canoes so numerous that even though we use cannon they could readily overwhelm us.

I have seldom felt more alone than at this moment, knowing that our safety may now depend more upon the manner in which I face them than upon the weapons we can bring to bear. Whatever happens tomorrow, whatever the aggravation with which I am faced, I must not lose my temper, but must act as though I had a power over them . . .

I have just been on deck, having heard Musket fire from the shore where we have our tents and Observatory. It is now almost Midnight and this is the second time the centry there has opened fire, the first time being about 10 p.m. All is quiet again now and I pray Mr King and his people are not overwhelmed in the night. I have ordered a sharp lookout kept and the boats to be held ready But I do believe matters have not yet reached the point where a show of force and my own presence are no longer sufficient to keep the situation within my control, and it will not be long now before we are at sea again.

The diary or personal record ends there.
The next day Cook was dead.

PART SEVEN

Cook's Death

It was Sunday, 14th February, 1779, and what happened ashore that morning in Hawaii is covered by most of those who kept journals. In describing the manner of his death I have drawn particularly on the Journal of Captain Clerke who succeeded to command of the expedition.

HAMMOND INNES

It was the theft of the *Discovery*'s cutter that started the events that led to Cook's death. At daybreak that Sunday morning Lt Burney, Officer of the Watch on board of the *Discovery*, observed the cutter no longer sunk at her mooring buoy and reported its disappearance to Capt Clerke. Close examination revealed that the 4"-rope securing it to the buoy had been cut. The fact that it had been filled with water, to tighten up the planking which had been opened by the heat of the sun, had made the theft easier, the look-out being unable to see the sunken hull in the dark. In view of the previous day's trouble Clerke reported the loss to his Commander, and, after some discussion, he and Cook agreed that the *Discovery*'s boats should head for the SE point of the Bay and the *Resolution*'s for the NW point with the object of seizing all the native canoes and holding them until the cutter had been returned.

The time was then something before 7 a.m.

According to King, who had come out to the *Resolution* to report that natives had been seen skulking round the shore base during the night, Capt Clerke was 'too unwell to go on shore to Terreeoboo'. Burney, the 1st Lieutenant of the *Resolution*, says much the same thing, that Capt Cook 'desired Captain Clerke to go on shore to the old King Terreeoboo, to endeavour to prevail on him to use his authority and influence to have the boat restored. Captain Clerke was in too reduced a state of health for so much exertion, and was obliged to excuse himself.'

Cook was well aware of Clerke's condition and since King reports that when he came on board of the *Resolution* 'they were all arming themselves & the Captn loading his double Barreld piece' it is likely that the instant Cook heard of the theft he had decided to go himself and had already made up his mind to seize the king as a hostage as well as any canoes the boats could lay their hands on.

Clerke returned to his ship and sent Lt Rickman away in his two remaining boats, a launch and a cutter, with their crews and some marines, all well armed, to the SE of the Bay. After seeing them on their way, he had himself rowed back to the *Resolution* in the jolly boat with the intention of discussing the matter further with Capt Cook. On arrival he was informed that Cook had himself gone ashore in the pinnace, accompanied by the launch and small cutter, and had headed straight for Kaawaloa, the town or large village on the NW point where King Terreeoboo lived. Clerke then returned to his ship in the belief that everything would be all right and that the cutter would be quickly recovered once Cook had seen the King.

Everything at that time seemed reasonably normal with quite a few small canoes trading with the ships. However, shortly after his return, Clerke heard musket fire from his own boats and sent the jolly boat away to the SE to discover the cause of it, which he could not see from the *Discovery*, and also to bring back any captured canoes. It was most probably the news that they had shot and killed an Aree, or chief, named Kareemoo that was the cause of all that followed. The time was then just on 8 a.m. and shortly afterwards those on board the two ships heard a volley of shots and a great uproar from the mass of natives gathered around Cook's boats at the NW point opposite the town of Kaawaloa. Clerke, looking through his telescope, says that he could clearly see 'our People were drove off to their Boats'.

He could not see Cook or identify any individual. But his first lieutenant, Burney, who was on deck beside him looking through his own glass, says he could 'see Capt Cook receive a Blow from a Club and fall off a Rock into the Water'.

At this time both the pinnace and the launch were firing and the *Resolution*, which was moored close off the landing beach, opened fire, throwing shot into the crowd milling around the beach. With all their boats away there was nothing else the ships could do and Clerke had to look helplessly on until the shore engagement was called off for lack of ammunition and Lt Williamson, who was in command of the boats, had reported to him from the *Resolution*. It was then that he heard definitely that Cook was dead and himself now the Commander of the Expedition.

He immediately transferred to the *Resolution* and despatched a strong force to protect the observatory and all that were ashore working on the mast. Four marines had been killed and three wounded, including Phillips, their 2nd Lieutenant, who had been stabbed in the shoulder with an iron spike and was badly bruised with stones. It was Phillips who gave Clerke a blow-by-blow account of what had happened, and though it is inevitably a little confused in places it is the most personal information we shall ever have of the untimely and quite unnecessary death of England's greatest navigator.

Capt Cook landed at the Town situate within the NW point with his Pinnace & Launch, leaving the small Cutter off the Point to prevent the escape of any Canoes that might be dispos'd to get off, at his Landing he order'd 9 Marines which we had in the Boats and myself onshore to attend him and immediately march'd into the Town where he enquired for Terre'oboo and the 2 Boys (his sons had liv'd principally with Capt Cook onboard the Resolution since Terre'oboo's first arrival among us). Messengers were immediately dispatch'd and the 2 Boys soon came and conducted us to their Fathers house.

After waiting some time on the outside Capt Cook doubted the old Gentlemans being there and sent me in that I might inform Him. I found our old acquaintance just awoke from Sleep when upon my acquainting him that Capt Cook was at the door, he very readily went with me to Him. Capt Cook after some little conversation observ'd that Terre'oboo was quite innocent of what had happen'd and proposed to the old Gentleman to go onboard with him, which he readily agreed to, and we accordingly proceeded towards the Boats, but having advanc'd near to the Water side an elderly Woman whose name was Kar'na'cub'ra one of his Wives came to him and with many tears and intreaties beg'd he would not go onboard, at the same time 2 Chiefs laid hold of him and insisting that he should not, made him sit down, the old Man now appear'd dejected and frighten'd.

It was at this period we first began to suspect that they were not very well dispos'd towards us, and the Marines being huddled together in the midst of an immense Mob compos'd of at least 2 or 3 thousand People, I propos'd to Capt Cook that they might be arrang'd in order along the Rocks by the Water side which he approving of, the Crowd readily made way for them and they were drawn up accordingly: we now clearly saw they were collecting their Spears &c, but an Artful Rascal of a Priest was singing & making a ceremonious offering of a Coco Nut to the Capt and Terre'oboo to divert their attention from the Manoeuvres of the surrounding multitude.

Capt Cook now gave up all thoughts of taking Terre'oboo onboard with the following observation to me, 'We can never think of compelling him to go onboard without killing a number of these People,' and I believe was just

going to give orders to embark, when he was interrupted
by a fellow arm'd with a long Iron Spike (a pahoa, or
dagger) and a Stone; this Man made a flourish with his
Pah'hoo ah, and threaten'd to throw his stone upon which
Capt Cook discharg'd a load of small shot at him but he
having his Mat on the small shot did not penetrate it,
and had no other effect than farther to provoke and
encourage them, I could not observe the least fright it
occasion'd; immediately upon this an Aree arm'd with a
Pah'hoo'ah attempted to stab me but I foil'd his attempt
by giving him a severe blow with the Butt End of my
Musket, just at this time they began to throw stones,
and one of the Marines was knock'd down, the Capt
then fir'd a ball and kill'd a Man.

They now made a general attack and the Capt gave
orders to the Marines to fire and afterwards called out
'Take to the Boats'. I fir'd just after the Capt and loaded
again whilst the Marines fir'd; almost instantaneously
upon my repeating the Orders to take to the Boats I was
knock'd down by a stone and in rising receiv'd a Stab
with a Pah'hoo'ah in the shoulder, my Antagonist was
just upon the point of seconding his blow when I shot him
dead, the business was now a most miserable scene of
confusion – the Shouts and Yells of the Indians far exceeding all the noise I ever came in the way of, these fellows
instead of retiring upon being fir'd at, as Capt Cook and I
believe most People concluded they would, acted so very
contrary a part, that they never gave the Soldiers time to
reload their Pieces but immediately broke in upon and
would have kill'd every man of them had not the Boats
by a smart fire kept them a little off and pick'd up those
who were not too much wounded to reach them.

After being knock'd down I saw no more of Capt Cook,
all my People I observ'd were totally vanquish'd and

endeavouring to save their lives by getting to the Boats –
I therefore scrambled as well I could into the Water and
made for the Pinnace which I fortunately got hold of,
but not before I receiv'd another blow from a stone just
above the Temple which had not the Pinnace been very
near would have sent me to the Bottom.

This account, which I give in full because it is the only one
we have from a witness at close hand, cannot be taken entirely at its face value since Lt Phillips knew perfectly well
that at home it would be thoroughly scrutinised for any
evidence of failure on the part of his marines to do their
duty and protect the Commander of the expedition with
courage and discipline. And though Midshipman Harvey
supports him, another midshipman, Watts, gives a somewhat different view of the marines' behaviour. 'In the mean
time,' he writes in his journal, 'the Marines with the same
undisciplined infatuation began a fire also and the Attack
on both sides became general.' Watts claims that the 'undisciplined' firing by the marines was after Cook had waved
his hand at the boats and ordered them to stop firing – they
had apparently opened fire immediately the huge crowd
had started stone-slinging. He also says that it was whilst
Cook was getting down the beach to the boats to stop the
firing that he was stabbed 'somewhere near the shoulder
blade upon which he staggered a few paces and fell into the
Water where two or three of the Natives Jumped upon him
and beat him about the head with Stones until he expired.'
Samwell, who had been promoted to surgeon in the
Discovery six months previously and who, like Anderson
before him, kept a very full journal, is even more damning
in his comments on the behaviour of the marines. He says
that after the first volley the natives fell back and a 'vigorous
push at this juncture would have put them to flight; but

no sooner had the Marines made the general discharge but the body of them flung down their pieces and threw themselves into the water, on this all was over . . .'

He makes the point that natives of the Pacific, however numerous, will never stand and fight in the face of a group of 'resolute Men with fire arms who will firmly maintain their Ground.' He not only blames the marines for not standing their ground, but like Bayly and Watts, who refer specifically to Lt Williamson's order forbidding the boats, other than the cutter, to close the shore, even to embark men that were in the water, he finds it extraordinary that the three boats, which were all under the command of the *Resolution*'s 3rd Lieutenant and contained upwards of 40 seamen, most of them armed, did not take more resolute action. Thus Williamson's part in the affair becomes even more irresolute and unsatisfactory than the marines.

Something of Cook's sublime confidence in his ability to maintain command of the situation is indicated by Harvey's statement that when Phillips informed him that the natives were arming, which was surely something he could see for himself, 'the Captn made light of the intelligence, and from his actions, I imagine he thought that they were only arming themselves to act upon the defensive, that is to say, to protect the King from being taken off by force.' Again, when Phillips kept urging him to embark Cook merely agreed to his drawing his marines up on the rocks of the foreshore and himself still standing there 'permitted the greatest insults from them to such a degree that for the security of his own person he was obliged to shoot two of them . . . even after this by an infatuation that is altogether unaccountable he continued to trifle away his time on shore and did not attempt to recover the Boats until the attack was begun . . .'

Clearly Cook was not 'trifling away his time'. Throughout three expeditions he had succeeded in dominating every situation that had faced him and in the Pacific had grown accustomed to the excitability of the native peoples. Usually his own presence had proved sufficient to quieten them, particularly when backed up by a show of strength. Use of firearms had been a final resort and this had never failed, but in this instance, though he had ordered the marines to load their muskets with ball before leaving the ship, he had loaded one barrel of his own twin-barrelled piece with shot. It was this barrel that he fired first and since the man he fired at was wearing a protective mat, which was their armour against slung stones, it had no effect. His action was thus discredited in the eyes of the mob. They are reported as laughing at it, so that instead of subduing them, it only served to embolden them. Edgar, the *Discovery*'s master, is probably right in saying that 'had Capt Cooke come down to the boats directly as he was advised he most probably would have saved his life . . .' But it was not in Cook's nature to run from a native mob, and if he thought it an ugly situation and one that might get out of hand, the more reason for him to stay and outface them.

That it was an error of judgment is obvious, but I do not believe it was caused by fatigue. This is a recurrent theory, that Cook's judgment was impaired at this time by exhaustion due to the 8 years he had spent in arduous ocean exploration, and particularly by his disappointing and wearying voyage into the Arctic. My own sea experience gives me a little understanding of the nervous tension and fatigue that results from inshore navigation on a hostile and unfamiliar coast in poor weather conditions, but I also know the recovery rate, and Cook had had plenty of time to relax and unwind after the strain of navigating to the edge of the Arctic pack ice. The increased irascibility revealed in his official Journal is not in my view due either to fatigue or age, but to his feeling of frustration at having to spend another winter in the islands, and also to his growing facility in the use of words and the sense that he now had sufficient standing to express his irritation officially, even to the extent of criticising yard officers senior to himself.

Nor do I think it true to say that Cook was unaware of the almost godly status accorded him by the priests and the extent to which the resources of the island had been plundered to support his ships. He was not a sensitive man; few sailors are, their lives being mainly concerned with practicalities, and Cook in particular had spent the last 17 years largely immersed in the exact science of surveying and charting. But he certainly was not unaware of the strain his ships had imposed on the islands' economy and resources and the effect upon the people of his sudden and almost immediate return after the elaborate farewells.

That Cook was a changed man, however, I accept. Not in any fundamental sense, of course, but there is no doubt that on this third voyage his reactions to things were different, and they were different because his whole attitude, even his objectives, had been changed by the year he had spent ashore in England. He was a more ambitious man, or rather he was ambitious in a wider sense. His election to the Royal Society had opened new doors and prospects, and the time he had spent learning to write up his Journal for publication under the tutelage of Dr Douglas had given his precise and determined mind a new direction.

Like most eminently successful men, Cook possessed that quality of single-purposed drive that can ride roughshod over all opposition, sometimes with complete disregard for the feelings of others. On the enforced return to Kealakekua Bay his concern was the repair of the mast, nothing else. He was urgent to get to sea again, to explore Kamchatka and the Russian coast and make an earlier and more thorough search for the North West Passage. The grumblings of his own men on not being allowed ashore, the reluctance of the Hawaiian people to continue to supply his ships and their thieving propensities all served to increase his irascibility. He was never the easiest of men and his temper could be very short indeed. At times he could be quite unfeeling. The punishment of men meant nothing to him so long as it was deserved and for the good of the ship, or in the case of a native for the advantage of the expedition. The theft of the cutter, which could not readily be replaced and was essential to his operations in the north, was the last straw – in modern terminology he blew his top and went storming ashore, determined to put an end to these constant pinpricks by seizing upon the person of the King as a hostage.

The fact that he took only 9 marines with him out of a total of 31 is a measure of his hastiness and his supreme confidence in his ability to carry out his purpose by his own presence and if necessary a small show of force. And in this he would undoubtedly have been successful had not the news of Rickman's action with the *Discovery*'s boat at the south east point and the death of one of their chiefs been brought to Kaawaloa just as Cook was leading the old King to the boat. It was this which sent the king's wife rushing to her husband with entreaties to him not to go on board and others of his entourage to restrain him from proceeding. Up to that point everything was so normal that one of the King's two sons was already in the boat, and only left it on the advice of the sailors after the firing had started, for the pair of them spent a good deal of their time playing about on the *Resolution* and were very popular with the men.

Samwell with his eye on publication gives by far the most vivid and poignant account of Cook's death, but since he was on board of the *Discovery*, which was stationed further from the scene than the *Resolution*, we must accept that the account is based on general talk and conversations he may have had with those seamen who were in the boats. This is his account of Cook's end:

Captain Cook was advanced a few paces before the Marines when they fired, the Stones flew as thick as hail which knocked the Lieut. down & as he was rising a fellow stuck him in the back with a Spear, however he recovered himself shot the Indian dead and escaped into the Water.

Captain Cook was now the only Man on the Rock, he was seen walking down towards the Pinnace holding his left hand against the Back of his head to guard it from the Stones & carrying his Musket under the other Arm. An Indian came running behind him, stopping once or twice as he advanced, as if he was afraid that he should turn round, then taking him unaware he sprung to him, knocked him on the back of his head with a large Club taken out of a fence, & instantly fled with the greatest precipitation; the blow made Captain Cook stagger two or three paces, he then fell on his hand & one knee & dropped his Musket, as he was rising another Indian came running to him & before he could recover himself from the Fall drew out an iron Dagger he concealed under his feathered Cloak & stuck it with all his force into the back of his Neck, which made Captain Cook tumble into the Water in a kind of a bite by the side of the rock where the water is about knee deep; here he was followed by a crowd of people who endeavoured to keep him under water, but struggling very strong with them he got his head up & looking towards the Pinnace which was not above a boat hook's Length from him he waved his hands to them for Assistance, which it seems it was not in their Power to give.

The Indians got him under water again but he disengaged himself & got his head up once more & not being able to swim he endeavoured to scramble on the Rock, when a fellow gave him a blow on the head with a large Club and he was seen alive no more.

They now kept him under water, one man sat on his Shoulders & beat his head with a stone while others beat him with Clubs & Stones, taking a Savage pleasure in using every barbarity to the dead body; as soon as one had struck him another would take the Instrument out of his Body and give him another Stab.

The disparity between the various versions of what happened ashore that day is clearly due to the fact that the only man on the spot who wrote an account of it had reasons for representing his own men in the most favourable light. All the others wrote from hearsay and what they had observed of the confusion ashore from a distance. There is no doubt, however, that Cook's death was the result of his failure to appreciate fully the changed mood of the Hawaiians and of course to the violence of his own reaction to the theft of the cutter. This quick temper of his, exacerbated in this instance by the frustration he felt at having to put back to the same bay and deal once again with the same people, emerges very strongly in the first biography of the navigator written by Andrew Kippis and published only nine years after his death.

Describing Cook's character and getting much of his information from Banks and Samwell, Kippis writes: 'With the greatest benevolence and humanity of disposition, Captain Cook was occasionally subject to hastiness of temper. This, which has been exaggerated by the few (and they are indeed few) who are unfavourable to his memory, is acknowledged by his friends.'

Elaborating on Cook's character he quotes firstly from King, by then a Captain: 'The constitution of his body was robust, inured to labour and capable of undergoing the severest hardship. His stomach bore, without difficulty, the coarsest and most ungrateful foods; great was the indifference to which he submitted to every kind of self-denial. The qualities of his mind were of the same hardy and vigorous kind as those of his body. His understanding was strong and perspicacious. His judgment, in whatever related to the services he was engaged in, was quick and sure. His designs were bold and manly and, both in conception and in the mode of execution, bore evident marks of a great original genius. His courage was cool and determined, and accompanied by an admirable presence of mind in the moment of danger. His temper might perhaps have been justly blamed, as subject to hastiness and passion, had not these been disarmed by a disposition the most benevolent and humane.'

Kippis also quotes Samwell on Cook – 'His constitution was strong; his mode of living temperate. He was a modest man, and rather bashful; of an agreeable lively conversation sensible and intelligent. In his temper he was somewhat hasty, but of a disposition the most friendly, benevolent, and humane. His person was about six feet high and, though a goodlooking man, he was plain both in address and appearance. His head was small, his hair, which was a dark brown, he wore tied behind. His face was full of expression; his nose exceedingly well shaped; his eyes, which were small and of a brown cast, were quick and piercing, his eyebrows prominent which gave his countenance altogether an air of austerity.'

Both men refer to his single-purposed determination. King writes: 'But the most distinguishing feature (of Cook's character) was that unremitting perseverance in the pursuit of his object, which was not only superior to the opposition of dangers, and the pressure of hardships, but even exempt from the want of ordinary relaxation. During the long and tedious voyages in which he was engaged, his eagerness and activity were never in the least abated. No incidental temptation could detain him for a moment; even those intervals of recreation which sometimes unavoidably occurred and were looked for by us with a longing that persons who have experienced fatigues of service will readily excuse, were submitted to by him with a certain impatience, whenever they could not be employed in making a further provision for the more effective prosecution of his design.'

Samwell puts it more elaborately: 'With a clear judgment, strong masculine sense, and most determined resolution – with a genius peculiarly turned for enterprise, he pursued his object with unshaken perseverence; – vigilant and active in an eminent degree; – cool and intrepid among dangers; patient and firm under difficulties and stress; fertile in expedients; great and original in all his designs; active and resolved in carrying them into execution.'

These examples give some indication of how he was regarded by those he commanded. No seaman ever had better epitaphs by those who sailed with him.

PART EIGHT

The End
of the Voyage

Captain Clerke's initial and natural reaction, on succeeding to the command of the expedition, was to send a force ashore, burn the town and avenge Cook's death. But after thinking it over, he came to the more sensible conclusion that any further loss of men would be to the detriment of the voyage. He posted Lt Gore to the command of the *Discovery* and having got the mast aboard and all the men that were ashore re-embarked, set about getting the *Resolution* fit for sea as soon as possible.

His acceptance of the situation without any reprisals was not to the liking of his men. It was bad enough seeing a chief parading ashore with Cook's hanger, or sword, but when another of them came out in a canoe and had himself paddled around the ships flaunting Cook's hat on his head and slapping his backside in contempt of the sailors, they went to Clerke in a body and requested revenge. He agreed to land a force and burn the town, but this had to be postponed as Gore was not ready to have the *Discovery* warped in to cover the landing.

There followed almost a week of provocation by the natives and periodic skirmishing ashore due to the fact that water had to be brought off to the ships. The native weapon was the sling, and so ignorant were they of firearms that, because of the flame and smoke, they thought they were being killed by burning and as a protection soaked their body armour of mats with water. All this time the *Resolution* was very vulnerable to attack, her decks being littered with spars and cordage, but the *Discovery*, with two more guns brought up from the hold, was warped in to cover the watering and on February 17 Kealakekua, the village nearest the watering point, was set on fire, some 50 or 60 houses being destroyed including that of the priest who had been their most consistent friend. Feeling among the men ran so high that the heads of two of the natives they had killed were cut off and mounted in the boats lying off to protect the watering parties.

All this time Clerke was endeavouring to recover Cook's remains, the Hawaiians repeatedly trying to lure him or his officers ashore to receive them. In the end they appear to have become frightened that further reprisals would be taken and on Saturday the 20th they made their peace, handing in to the pinnace a large bundle wrapped in a cloak of black and white feathers. This bundle, which contained all that remained of Cook's body, was unwrapped in the great cabin of the *Resolution*, and Samwell, who presumably examined it in his capacity as surgeon, gives the following descriptions of its contents:

We found in it the following bones with some flesh upon them which had the marks of fire. The Thighs & Legs joined together but not the feet, both Arms with the Hands seperated from them, the Skull with all the bones that form the face wanting with the Scalp seperated from it, which was also in the bundle with the hair on it cut short, both Hands whole with the Skin of the fore Arms joined to them, the hands had not been in the fire, but were salted, several Gashes being cut in them to take the Salt in. Tho we had no doubt concerning the Identity of any of the parts contained in the bundle, every one must be perfectly satisfied as to that of the hands, for we all knew the right by a large Scar on it seperating for about an inch the Thumb from the forefinger. The Ears adhered to the Scalp, which had a cut in it about an inch long, probably from the first blow he received with the Club, but the Skull was not fractured so that it is likely that the Stroke was not mortal.

That same day the *Resolution*'s mast was stepped. On the Sunday Cook's hanger was brought out to the *Resolution*, also the 2 barrels of his gun which 'had been taken asunder and the end of one of them beaten flat intended to be made into Daggers or small adzes.' The following day his under-jaw and feet were delivered, together with his shoes and a bit of his hat. And on that day Monday, February 22, just one week after his clothes had been sold in the great cabin to his fellow officers as is still the custom in the Navy, what was left of Cook was committed to the deep 'with all attention and honour we could possibly pay it in this part of the World.' At 5 in the afternoon both ships had their ensigns and pennants flying at half mast, their yards crossed, and at 5.45 the *Resolution* tolled her bell and fired a 20 gun salute in slow time as the remains were slid over the side into the Pacific.

The following day Clerke sailed in an endeavour to succeed where Cook had failed the previous year, and before their departure the ships were once again crowded with Hawaiians, gifts being exchanged and all on the friendliest terms, even girls living aboard. He spent three weeks exploring the remainder of the Hawaiian Group and then headed for the coast of Kamchatka, which he reached on April 23 after a night of frost, snow and sleet.

He was too ill to explore ashore as Cook would have done, but he sent his officers, and while the ships were making up the river to Petropavlovsk the Governor, Major Behm, paid him a visit. This most helpful and generous official, who was later treated so callously by his government and Prince Potemkin in particular, was on the point of returning to St Petersburg. To him Clerke entrusted Cook's journal for delivery to the English Ambassador, also reports from King and Bayly and his own journal since succeeding to command. By this means, and after an interval of 7 months, the news of Cook's death reached the Admiralty in London.

Clerke remained with his ships harboured at Petropavlovsk for the better part of a month, sailing on June 16, having got on board the stores he needed, much of which were at Major Behm's personal expense. By the first day of July he was into the Gulf of Anadir, through the Bering Straits by July 6, and from July 7 to July 27 he probed northwards, all the time either in the ice or on the edge of the pack. But at no time did he get further north than Cook.

On Wednesday, July 21, he wrote in his journal: 'It is now clearly impossible to proceed in the least farther to the Noward upon this Coast and it is equally as improbable that this amazing mass of Ice should be dissolv'd by the few remaining Summer weeks which will terminate this Season but it doubtlessly remain as it now is a most unsurmountable barrier to every attempt we can possibly make. I therefore think it the best step I can take for the good of the service to trace the Ice over to the Asiatic Coast, try if I can find a Hole that will admit me any further North, if not see whats to be done upon that Coast where I hope but cannot much flatter myself with meeting better success, for this Sea is now so Choak'd with Ice that a passage I fear is totally out of the question.'

This was his last journal entry. He had pushed himself and his ships to the limit and was totally exhausted. He turned south, was back through the Bering Straits on July 30, and the day after they sighted the coast of Kamchatka again he was dead. He had been totally confined to his bed since August 16 and died at 8.30 a.m. on August 22. It is a pity Anderson was not alive, or somebody on board to give a proper obituary to so conscientious a man. In King's recently discovered Journal the entry for August 22 reads: 'Captn Clerke dyed on the 22nd Augst. when we were almost in sight of the bay of Awatshka; his disorder was a consumption* of which he had lingered during the whole voyage & his decay was so gradual, that he did the duty of his station till within a week of his death, when being no longer able to come on deck, he desired the officers to receive my orders & gave the command up to me . . .' Later King wrote what can be described as a brief obituary: 'He had three times encircled the World, & attempted a fourth, In the pursuit of which for the last half year, he commanded the expedition, nor did he swerve in any instance from persevering on account of his health, preferring his duty to his Country, to even his own life.'

Samwell, though a surgeon, is less than generous in his final comment, but does give a fair character sketch:

Captn Clerke was a sensible Man & a good Sailor, but did not possess that degree of Firmness & Resolution necessary to constitute the Character of a great Commander. He was ever diffident of himself & consequently wavering and unfixed in his Conduct, except where a certain Line of Action was chalked out to him & then no man was readier to pursue it than himself; he was fitter to be second than first in Command, fitter to execute than to plan. However his Perseverance in pursuing the Voyage after the death of Captn Cook, notwithstanding his own

---

* King himself was to die of consumption in November 1784 aged 34.

bad state of Health will ever reflect Honour upon his Memory. The most remarkable part of his Character was his happy convivial Turn & humourous Conversation in which he excelled most Men; these, joined to an open generous Disposition, made his Company universally caressed and engaged him in excesses which laid the Foundation of the Complaint of which he died.

Thus both Commanders were lost in a voyage that finally extended to 4 years and 3 months. But in spite of all the ships had been through, indifferently rigged and fitted out, ranging the Pacific, exploring new islands and the northern coasts of America and Asia, and twice spending weeks on the edge of the Arctic pack ice for which they were not equipped, they only lost 12 men of a total complement of 194, including those who joined at the Cape. Of this total only 5 died of disease during the voyage, and in the case of Clerke at any rate this was from tuberculosis which he had contracted before sailing A great tribute to Cook's routine of hygiene, something that was not fully recognised at the time and is one of the most important aspects of this and his earlier voyages.

His achievements as a navigator, however, were recognised, both in his own country and abroad. The standing and regard with which he was held in England is indicated by the official reaction to the news of his death. The Royal Society had commemorative medals struck in gold and silver with Cook's head in profile and round it Jac. Cook Oceani Investigator Acerrimus; and on the reverse Britannia holding a globe and the words: Nil Intentatum Nostri Liquere, Auspiciis Georgii III. One of the gold medals was given to Mrs Cook. The King granted her a pension of £200 a year and £25 a year to each of her three sons, also a family coat of arms. And the Admiralty allocated the profits of the book of the voyage* almost entirely to the families of those officers who were dead by the time it was published, one half going to Mrs Cook and her family, a quarter to King's heirs, an eighth to Clerke's and the remaining eighth to Bligh, less 100 guineas to Anderson's heirs; a most unusual action by a Board that was never distinguished for its generosity.

Abroad his standing was such that though France had joined the United States in their war against England, both countries ordered their warships to grant safe conduct to the *Resolution* and the *Discovery*. Benjamin Franklin instructed his privateers: *A Ship having been fitted out from England, before the Commencement of this War, to make Discoveries of new Countries in unknown Seas, under the Conduct of the most celebrated Navigator and Discoverer Captain Cook* ... he earnestly entreated them to *treat the said Captain Cook and his people with all Civility and Kindness, affording them as common Friends to Mankind all the Assistance in your Power which they may happen to stand in need of.* These instructions were signed *B. Franklin, Minister Plenipotentiary from the Congress of the United States at the Court of France.*

Finally, Sir Joseph Banks, who as President of the Royal Society had sent the gold medal to Mrs Cook with a note saying 'His name will live for ever', initiated and encouraged Kippis to write his biography. This was the first of the many volumes that have been written about Captain James Cook RN in the 200 years since he was killed in Hawaii. In 1874 a concrete obelisk was erected in Kealakekua Bay; and in 1928

* *A Voyage to the Pacific Ocean* ... was published in 1784, the first two volumes being credited to Cook, the third to King. The first edition priced at 4½gns sold out in 3 days. The second and third editions did not appear until 1785 by which time the first edition was changing hands at 10gns. The Cook family share of the profits according to Prof. Beaglehole, 'certainly amounted to over £2,000.'

a small bronze plaque was set into the seabed below the water near the spot where he fell. But his real memorial is the great multiplicity of islands, headlands and bays he discovered and named, the charts he drew and the work of the naturalists and painters who sailed with him.

* * * *

AUTHOR'S NOTE

This self-revealing account of Cook's search for the North West Passage, written as a diary or personal record of the great navigator's last tragic voyage, is something that I feel is within the bounds of possibility. Even his official journal, so different from those of the two previous voyages, reveals his newly awakened interest in writing.

In presenting the main body of this work as Cook's own writing I am conscious of having taken a great liberty for which I hope those who are as fascinated by the subject as I am will forgive me. I have done it for two reasons:

Apart from my writing, I have had sixteen years of sailing my own boat on the coasts of Europe. I know the sea at close quarters and as a result I felt it was possible to imagine myself standing in Cook's shoes on board of the *Resolution*. Also, in my travels I have gone out of my way over the years to visit places that Cook visited, even his passage through the Great Barrier Reef and the almost inaccessible Dusky Bay in New Zealand. The fact is that I seem to have been living with Cook a very long time now.

Captain Cook's journals tell us nothing about the man himself. They are official journals, as were those written by the men who sailed with him. If, therefore, I have succeeded to any degree at all in bringing this great navigator to life I shall be happy, the work having been done as a labour of love and in an honest endeavour to set right the impression left by those official journals. Cook was neither a dull man, nor unemotional and inhuman. He could not have been, or he would not have achieved what he did.

Addendum

Apart from my indebtedness to the late Professor J. C. Beaglehole for the years of dedicated research that has made this book possible, I would also like to express my thanks to Dr Helen Wallis, Map Librarian of the British Library, for finding the time, in the midst of preparing her paper on Captain Cook for the Vancouver Symposium, to check my manuscript and put me right on a number of points. It was Dr Wallis who informed me that Captain King's journal for the latter part of this voyage has only recently come to light after 200 years – among Miscellaneous Sailing Directions at the Hydrographic Department, Taunton. A most extraordinary coincidence!

Hammond Innes

'If you are looking for a tough action novel, of man against the elements, breathless but credible, out of the ordinary but authentic, you can't do better than a good Hammond Innes.' *Richard Lister, Evening Standard*

'Hammond Innes has a real genius for conveying atmosphere.' *Daily Telegraph*

THE BIG FOOTPRINTS 95p
AIR BRIDGE £1.25
ATLANTIC FURY £1.25
ATTACK ALARM £1.25
THE BLUE ICE 85p
CAMPBELL'S KINGDOM £1.25
THE DOOMED OASIS 85p
THE LAND GOD GAVE TO CAIN £1.25
LEVKAS MAN £1.00
THE LONELY SKIER £1.00
MADDON'S ROCK £1.00
THE STRANGE LAND 85p
THE STRODE VENTURER 85p
THE TROJAN HORSE £1.00
THE WHITE SOUTH £1.25

Fontana Paperbacks

Fontana Paperbacks

Fontana is a leading paperback publisher of fiction and non-fiction, with authors ranging from Alistair MacLean, Agatha Christie and Desmond Bagley to Solzhenitsyn and Pasternak, from Gerald Durrell and Joy Adamson to the famous Modern Masters series.

In addition to a wide-ranging collection of international popular writers of fiction, Fontana also has an outstanding reputation for history, natural history, military history, psychology, psychiatry, politics, economics, religion and the social sciences.

All Fontana books are available at your bookshop or newsagent; or can be ordered direct. Just fill in the form and list the titles you want.

FONTANA BOOKS, Cash Sales Department, G.P.O. Box 29, Douglas, Isle of Man, British Isles. Please send purchase price, plus 8p per book. Customers outside the U.K. send purchase price, plus 10p per book. Cheque, postal or money order. No currency.

NAME (Block letters)

ADDRESS
